Hot Quit

Hot Quit

KATHRYN ROBERTS

Montlake
Romance

The characters and events portrayed in this book are fictitious. Any similarity to real persons, living or dead, is coincidental and not intended by the author.

Published by Montlake Romance
P.O. Box 400818
Las Vegas, NV 89140

ISBN-13: 9781612186894
ISBN-10: 1612186890

This book is for my mother, Rose Marie Earhart,

who never gave up on my writing.

CHAPTER 1

The midday heat rippled the air, distorting the painted circle denoting the landing zone, giving it life as it waved and undulated at the top of a black and green glass skyscraper. From above, Alexandria Payne watched her perfectly proper personal secretary lose part of her composure as she fought her skirt swirling around her legs. The helicopter settled on the rooftop like a huge bird on its nest, and the moment the skids touched down, Alexandria sat back, gathered her briefcase, and systematically ordered her thoughts as she did every time she returned from a business trip.

As the rotor blades slowed, the copilot jumped from the cockpit and opened the passenger door. He was quick to offer his hand to Alexandria as she emerged and even quicker to reach inside for her bags as she stepped away.

"Please wait here until I call," she said with the air of a person accustomed to giving orders. "I'm sure that once I speak with Mr. Maitland, we'll want to dine…somewhere." She smoothed the side of her blonde hair, the Los Angeles heat already forcing a hint of perspiration on her brow as she turned to the older woman. "Hesperia. Did Mr. Maitland confirm the meeting with the COMJET people for tomorrow?"

"Yes, ma'am," she answered as she took the garment bag from the copilot. The helicopter engine stilled, leaving only the whoosh of the blades as they decelerated. "He has also arranged for you to dine with the Phelpses."

"No," Alexandria said as she strode toward the elevator. "He'll have to cancel. I don't have time to socialize now that we're so close to getting the upper hand with COMJET. He has to realize how important this is—well, never mind, I'll speak to him"—she strode ahead—"...did he check into..." The pair stepped into the elevator and the sound of her voice disappeared as the door slid shut. The helicopter blades stalled, and it was quiet except for the distant sound of ordinary life twenty stories below.

Minutes later, Alexandria sat behind her own desk—glad to be inside with air conditioning—and tried to concentrate on the figures before her. Some things just fell into place, and then there were others that were trouble from start to finish. The COMJET deal was one of the latter, but those were the ones that Alexandria lived for—they were the challenge; they were the sparks she needed to keep her sanity, to make life interesting. When she and Paul Maitland had entered into their partnership, she'd been the one to take risks, the daring one who plotted and schemed, and he'd been the solid fact-finder, the reliable one who found ways for her schemes to become reality.

That had been ten years ago, and today their APM Corporation was known worldwide as a player, as a formidable bidder in the high-dollar game of buying, selling, and reorganizing businesses and corporations.

COMJET was Alexandria's brainchild, and her latest conquest. Each piece of the puzzle was almost ready to fall into place, but there was one hitch. In order to market COMJET's innovative aeronautical product, it had to be shipped from a small midwestern town to a major transportation center. The only existing shipping line large enough to handle the job and located close enough to be cost effective was owned by a Texan who never sold anything cheap and who had already told Paul he wasn't interested in selling at any price.

Alexandria taxed her brain and tapped her manicured nails in momentary frustration, barely giving notice to Paul as he burst in through the private entrance to her office.

"I need to talk to you about this dinner with the Phelpses." He stood before her, arms crossed over his chest, destroying the clean lines of his Armani suit. He strolled to a leather side chair and sat. Alexandria smiled, appreciative of his confidence, but waiting, like a cat playing with a mouse, for him to wage his argument.

She ceased the drumroll on the desktop. "My trip was fine, thank you."

"Alexandria, come on, you've never been one to enjoy polite chitchat."

She sat quietly, but resumed clicking her nails, keeping a primitive kind of time against the polished wooden slab. "You think you know me pretty well, don't you?"

He rose, came to her side, tipped her chin up, and leaned over to caress her cheek with his lips. "Yes, Alexandria, I do know you, and I know you'll agree that we have to dine with the Phelpses tonight."

"Something going on?" She caught the sparkle in his eye and realized it wasn't going to be strictly a social affair. "What?" She rose and ran her palms over his lapels and lapped her fingers together around his neck. "Tell me. You know I detest secrets."

He smiled, his perfect teeth matching his perfectly barbered blond hair. "It's not secrets you dislike, Alexandria; it's secrets that you aren't privy to. But consider this. I think Howard is going to pop the question tonight, and if we were there to celebrate…"

"Say no more." Her hands dropped from his neck. "I see what you're getting at. Both ends of this budding marriage have wonderfully world-class banking connections."

Paul nodded. "Never turn your back on a friend. We might even be best man and maid of honor."

Alexandria sighed. "All right. But first sit down and tell me everything you've learned about our Texan friend. We have to figure out what to do about him before we go celebrate, or I won't enjoy my food at all."

"My thoughts exactly. Now..." He slid her chair up behind her, seating her. He sat down on the corner of her desk. "This man doesn't have any weak spots. He's financially as sound as anything I've ever seen, and I can't find anything he wants that he hasn't got. This company is his baby because it was the original. It was where he got his start."

"Are you sure there's nothing he wants? We only have sixty days to pull this together."

"Positive. He doesn't even care about operating his little empire; he's hired people to do it for him, and he just oversees the profits and losses and collects the earnings. He stays on his ranch, and from what I understand, you can't get him off a horse long enough to talk to him."

"Horses? He likes horses, then." Alexandria raised a perfectly formed brow.

"Cutting horses to be exact," he said.

"Well then," she agreed, "we'll find the best cutting horse in the world and use it to draw him in. Just what is a cutting horse?"

"Some foolishness about a rider separating one single cow from a whole herd of cows, and this guy already owns the best horses."

"Well then," Alexandria said, clenching her teeth behind a very insincere smile. "You'll ride into this old coot's backyard and let him find out you *love* cutting horses as much as he does. No contest. He'll give in."

"No." Paul stood up shaking his head. "Not me. I'm allergic to horses. I hate horses. You used to ride. You're better suited to this than I am."

"You're a Texan," Alexandria stated firmly.

"I left because I didn't like it."

"Well then, how old is this Texan?"

"Old enough to be your father, but he's single and looking," Paul smiled.

Alexandria sighed and moved toward the glass wall overlooking Los Angeles. "You sound like you'd agree to my getting friendlier with him."

Paul came up behind her and put his arms around her waist. "I wouldn't want you to do anything you didn't want to, but we do really need his help to pull COMJET off. He won't even answer phone calls or e-mails, so once you get close enough to talk to him face-to-face, I'm sure you will be able to persuade him to sell." He nuzzled her ear and pulled her closer. "You're so very good at everything you do."

Alexandria wondered. If she was so good at everything she did, how come it was never enough? How come she always wanted something more than she had? Right now, she wanted more from Paul. She could handle his wanting her to befriend an old geezer, but beyond that, she wanted him to hold her with no purpose in mind other than passion. She wanted real enthusiasm. They had been engaged for two years, but still, Alexandria couldn't rid herself of the feeling that she sat on the outside of his heart and was never going to be really close to his soul—or was it he that never really got to *her* heart and soul?

"Well," Paul jumped into her thoughts, "I think Hesperia needs to find a cutting horse trainer so you can ride right into this guy's mind and ownership of his trucking firm."

She pulled away but looked straight into his clear, beautiful blue eyes. *How hard could it be?* A few lessons to get the hang of it and she *could* ride into the Texan's life and get what she wanted. It was no different from any other acquisition. In fact, this would be more of a vacation than anything else, since she had been certifiably horse crazy at one time.

"All right. You owe me, though." She buzzed Hesperia. "I need you to find the best cutting horse trainer in the country.

Make arrangements with him to give me lessons and teach me everything he knows."

Except for the chicken scratching and pecking in the dirt and the idiot dog that ran barking at her car and tried to chew her tires as she drove in, there wasn't a soul around. The trainer's place was simple, but neat. A small wooden barn with paddocks faced an arena and a larger building Alexandria assumed to be another barn. A mobile home sat on top of a small hill at the end of the drive, surrounded by a cedar post and rail fence with manicured grass inside. It overlooked the arena and barns, and, as a whole, there was nothing out of place; every board, every rail fairly sparkled with homespun simplicity.

The dog continued to bark, the chicken continued to peck, and, if the stifling July heat weren't enough, Alexandria began to fume.

She was paying a small fortune to this trainer, and Hesperia had been quite clear about the time she was to arrive. Not only was there no one to meet her at Sacramento "International" Airport, but after waiting for hours, she gave in and rented a car. It was the only vehicle available, and the cheap little compact was a very loose interpretation of the word *car*. She'd driven more than an hour to get to Ione, the town closest to the ranch, and then another half hour to the ranch, over potholes, ruts, and gravel. Now having finally arrived, the only living thing that acknowledged her presence was an obsessed dog.

Exasperated, she slammed the heel of her palm against the horn, hoping the blast would outdo the dog and bring someone to her rescue.

Fifteen minutes later, she was sweltering, the dog had ceased barking, and a man in a straw hat ambled from the barn.

"Hel-loo!" Alexandria shouted and waved from the car. "Tell Jackson Morgan that Alexandria Payne is here."

The man returned a blank stare until he heard the name. "Señor Morgan—riding." He pointed toward the larger of the two barns.

"Well, go get him, please."

He shook his head slowly as if *she* were the one that didn't understand. "Señor Morgan—riding."

Alexandria smiled her best "go do it for me" smile, but the man just smiled back. It was obvious she was either going to have to go find Morgan herself or sit in this sauna of a car forever. She looked out the window. The dog was quietly staring at her like she was going to be his next meal. It was miserably hot, and she was in no mood to be intimidated by a dog.

Carefully she opened the door. The dog sat, like a guardian, in his spot near the front tire. Even more cautiously, Alexandria put one foot out, then the other. The dog tilted his head as if he were trying to understand her tedious progress. Finally she got out. The dog stood, turned, and walked away; she was no longer his concern.

Frustration raged in every muscle of her body, and despite a clear impression that she was losing her mind, she felt rejected by a mongrel dog. Slamming the car door, Alexandria headed toward the barn where she suspected Jackson Morgan could be found.

As soon as she entered the door, the cool smell of tanbark, shavings, and cows hit her. It took her eyes a moment to adjust to the shadows, but slowly a single rider came into focus. At the far end there was a small herd of about ten cows. The rider loped quietly in circles. His mount moved so fluidly that Alexandria could hear the horse's rhythmic breathing. A sudden and overwhelming sense of comfort and ease struck; slowly, she was mesmerized by the sight, the sound, and the feel of seclusion as the lone rider worked in a huge covered arena as if there were no one and nothing else on earth.

Alexandria had no clue how long she watched him ride. She saw him rein a thousand pounds of horseflesh into tighter and tighter circles as if he were a conductor guiding a symphony orchestra. In her mind she could hear and feel the ride growing to a crescendo like an emotional piece of music. She wanted to close her eyes and feel the power, but she was afraid she'd miss something.

The rider drew the horse into a tight spin, round and round, like a whirlwind gathering speed, like a Minotaur gone wild.

As suddenly and as smoothly as it had spun, the horse stopped. Alexandria realized she'd held her breath during the last moments of the show, and as the horse hung his head and blew, so did she. The rider patted the magnificent animal's neck almost lovingly. He grabbed hold of the thick, silky mane and pulled it playfully before moving the gelding forward.

The horse walked several steps toward Alexandria before the rider looked up and saw her. The spell was broken. There was no visible sign of recognition on his face as he drew closer. She fought the notion that her anger was no longer uppermost in her mind, and it irritated her. Without trying at all, he'd manipulated her so completely and so instantly into a passive, accepting state that was definitely not part of the Alexandria Payne she loved.

Narrowing her eyes, she stepped to the arena and rested her forearms on the top rail.

"Can I help you with something?" Jackson's voice was a deep, impatient, rather gravelly whisper that should have been irritating, but surprisingly was not. He stepped off the horse and stood before her.

Alexandria sized him up, something she'd learned to do quickly and automatically. He was tall—probably an inch or two over six feet, but it was hard to tell with boots. His shoulders were broad, hips deliciously narrow. He wore a baseball cap pulled down squarely across his forehead so that it was difficult to tell much about his eyes or his hair. That very fact made Alexandria more curious than she wanted to be.

"I'm Alexandria Payne," she announced.

"I'm Jackson Morgan," he returned after a long, pregnant pause. "Nice to meet you face-to-face, instead of through..."

Alexandria felt a comfortable kind of irritation build. "Hesperia, my private secretary. I thought she made arrangements for you to meet me at the airport."

"Private...secretary..." He nodded between words and his mouth twisted into a sly grin as if he were privy to a joke. "Well, if I had realized you wanted a chauffeur, I would have had Juan stop by on his way to pick up feed."

He dismounted, took one split rein, and led the horse toward the gate, leaving Alexandria. Instantly she made an uncomplimentary comparison between Morgan and his dog. She watched him exit the arena, halter the horse, and hand it to the man in the straw hat before he walked leisurely back to her.

"I expected—well, never mind, I want to know where to put my bags," she said as he passed.

He stood tall, facing her, the well-worn bridle hanging from his shoulder. "The bunkhouse."

"The bunkhouse?" All sorts of unwelcome images came to mind, including thin mattresses, metal-framed bunk beds, communal bathrooms, and the man she suspected was Juan. "I'm paying you seven thousand five hundred dollars for a month of training."

"Hesperia said you'd probably be staying in town."

"Yes, I'll have to talk to her about that. There is no suitable place in this small *town*, and although I haven't seen it yet, I'm reasonably certain that the bunkhouse won't do either."

He slapped his thigh with the end of the rein, then very slowly turned a devastatingly handsome smile on her. "Well, I have a small house; there's only one bed, but"—his smile deepened, revealing a dimple in one cheek and laugh lines around his dancing brown eyes—"I don't mind sharing if you don't."

"I do mind. You must have another room," Alexandria shot back quickly, used to bantering with sexual innuendoes.

"Yeah. There's another bedroom, but"—his smile grew wider—"it's an office, nothing but a couch."

"Very well, you can have the couch. Please show me where to put my bags." Alexandria spun on her heel and tried to get to her car before he had anything else to say. But she wasn't fast enough.

"No. 'Fraid that won't be the way it is." His voice became louder and some of the gravelly quality disappeared, leaving the sound of deep determination.

A battle of wills, is it? Alexandria turned back. "Fine. I'll find another trainer."

"No one better than me."

"If I can't work with you, what good is your expertise?" she parried, confident he'd give in.

"I told you I'd share," he returned with a sparkle in his eye.

"I'll find someone else." She turned and began to walk away again. She took several steps and thought he was going to let her go when she heard his gravelly whisper.

"Ten thousand."

She turned her head toward him to hear better. "What?"

His expression had changed. The sparkle had left his eye and the smile, although still there, was not the same. "Ten thousand dollars, in advance, and you can sleep in my bed— alone."

Alexandria's mind raced. His price was outrageous, but he *was* the best, and being a wheeler and dealer herself, she could appreciate the chance he was taking. But why? Either he was willing to sell himself and his bed or he wasn't. What difference did more money make when she was already paying dearly to get the best? Like a hawk searching for prey, her keen instincts told her that despite his casual treatment of the deal he offered, Jackson Morgan was not a man to sell himself. He needed the money. It was as simple as that, and in an instant, Alexandria knew she held the upper hand.

"All right. Ten thousand. You sleep in the bunkhouse."

He grinned again. "Nope. I'll take the couch in the office." He turned his back to her and began to walk away. "Give me fifteen minutes and you'll have your room."

She'd won, but that invigorating feeling wasn't quite there, and a tiny voice inside her questioned her success. "I'll be ready to ride in a half hour," she announced sharply, intent upon defining her place in this deal.

He stopped, turned to her, and smiled like he knew something she didn't. Every bit of confidence she'd just forced disappeared.

CHAPTER 2

"I thought Hesperia said you could ride a horse?" Jackson's voice boomed across the open arena as Alexandria loped down the rail. "You have to use your legs to cue him. That horse isn't going to work by mental telepathy. Gather him up with your reins and stop."

Alexandria's body cried out in pain, but she tried to squeeze her legs and sit down as she pulled the bay gelding to a stop. The instant she squeezed with her legs, the horse shot forward. To compensate, she used her hand harder and he stopped instantly, on his front end, jarring her to the bone and throwing her over his withers.

It was useless. There was nothing left of her to make another attempt. She dropped the reins and slumped in the saddle, wishing she could step off into a sauna and then on to one of Girta's fabulous whole-body massages. Paul was going to owe her big time for this. She was hot and sticky, and of all the things in the world she could be doing, this was not her first choice. Jackson's voice brought her back to reality.

"That musta shook every tooth in your head loose. A pile driver kind of stop like that is really hard to ride. You need to get him to sit down and slide."

Alexandria managed to turn her head enough to cast a scathing look at her tormentor, who strolled close enough to rest his hand on the bay horse's shoulder.

"You've been in the saddle an hour, and you're sloppy as hot bacon grease. How long *has* it been since you rode?"

As soon as she caught her breath enough to speak, Alexandria was going to answer, but for the moment, all she could do was suck in the hot San Joaquin Valley air and be thankful she was still mounted.

"I...well, I..." she gulped for breath.

Jackson watched her, no sign of mercy in his sour expression. "I *know* you haven't been on a horse lately, and by the way you use your hands, I know you've never been on a trained, *finished* horse."

Alexandria slid down from the saddle, secretly hoping her jellied legs would hold her weight, and faced him squarely. "I'll have you know I rode with Olympic hopefuls."

"Can I safely assume they're still hoping, or are they too old to get out of a wheelchair?"

Alexandria shot him her best steely, knock-'em-dead glare. "Several of them are now eventing in international circles and doing very well, I might add."

Jackson shook his head. "OK, so you rode English. Have you ever set a Western saddle before?"

"Well..." For the first time, Alexandria wondered just what Hesperia had told him. She searched for the appropriate answer. "Of course. I've been down into the Grand Canyon—"

"On vacation," he laughed a bit more rudely than called for. "I'm talking about working."

The man was infuriating, and Alexandria tried to laugh right back at him. "Work? You're trying to tell me about work?" She propped her hands on her hips to keep from lunging at his throat. "I'll tell you about work, Mr. Morgan. I have built a reputation for being tough and I didn't get it by 'vacationing.' I work fourteen-, sixteen-, and eighteen-hour days, and I *know* I can work circles around you. I'm paying you to teach me how to ride a cutting horse. Whatever Hesperia told you, and whatever my personal history is, it is none of your business and it has no bearing on our deal. You say you're the best, then prove it by teaching me."

Jackson raised one brow, but stood his ground under fire. She had spunk, and he liked a woman who could speak her mind. "You act like a green bronc on a cold morning. If you were to ask me, and I realize you haven't, I'd say you ought to calm down. Even if you had never been on a horse before, I *can* teach you to ride. I just need to know what I've got." His brown eyes focused on her. "You've just been assessed, Miss Payne."

Caught in the depths of his soft brown eyes, she narrowed her focus, directed a scathing glare at him, and tapped the toe of her brand-new boot in the dirt. She was unable to decide if he was speaking from a purely business standpoint or if he was toying with her. "And, Mr. Morgan, what have you decided?"

"You have potential." His face showed little emotion, but there was a sparkle in his eyes that she read as a challenge.

"Your hands and your legs need work, and you don't know much about riding faster than a walk, but you have a natural feel for the horse that will really come alive if you can ever figure out the timing and how to relax and let the horse do what he's supposed to. The first week we'll spend toughening you up, and I mean your body, Miss Payne, not your mind or that pretty little mouth of yours."

She began to say something, but he held his hand up and stopped her.

"The second week, we're going to put you on a few cows and see what you've learned. We might get you to a jackpot to let you face a little friendly competition, and the third week, I hope we can fix all the problems that crop up unexpectedly. The last week of your training, there is a pretty good sized cutting at Rancho

Temecula and we'll be working toward that as your goal. If you make it there, in front of our family of cutters, you'll be able to hold your own anywhere, provided you have a good horse under you. There won't be a minute to rest, and I can guarantee you that you'll be glad to hit the sack every night. Do you think you can take it?"

Alexandria breathed deep and smiled. "I can see why you've done well in your chosen field, Mr. Morgan. You get right to the point and I like that, but let me make it clear. I have a limited amount of time, and I'm no stranger to long hours. I may be from the city, but I am used to getting what I want; right now I want to ride a cutting horse."

His smile disappeared, and his gaze roved her face long enough for him to see how serious she was. "You're a tough nut. If you can stand the heat, we'll get along fine."

"Good. We finally understand each other." Alexandria punctuated her final word by flicking her thick blonde braid back over her shoulder—a childish move, but designed to show the proper amount of defiance. That defiance was calculated to hide the fact that inside, she was trembling from the confrontation. She had faced corporate magnates, bank presidents, and even generals without so much as a flicker of anxiety, but this trainer, this cowboy, seemed to be able to look right through her and settle somewhere between her very logical mind and her soul.

So far, she had struggled every moment to maintain her invincible-me attitude when he was around. She stared into his dark chocolate eyes and wondered if she was pulling off her act, infuriated since she was used to being the one who normally kept others wondering and on their toes. "We have a half hour before lunch," she said. "Do you want me back on the horse, Mr. Morgan?"

"Yes," Jackson said matter-of-factly as he nodded his head. "I want you to walk him out and cool him off—"

"You don't have grooms to do that?"

"No. You need to learn everything about how that horse feels, and from what I've seen, we've got a long way to go. I repeat, walk him out and cool him off good before you put him up. When he's cool, I want you to strip the saddle and put it back in the tack room, and then I want you to put the horse back in his stall after you brush him down. I also want you to stop calling me Mr. Morgan. Call me Jackson."

There is more than one way to skin a cat, Jackson thought as he declared himself the winner of this round. And Alexandria Payne was certainly a cat he'd enjoy skinning.

He watched her haul herself into the saddle even though her legs shivered in utter exhaustion. When she moved the horse away, he couldn't help but be more than a little impressed with her tenacity. She had a lot to learn, but she was gamy. If he'd pushed any other student as hard as he had pushed her in a couple of hours, they would have fallen apart and given up. He couldn't afford to spend a month with an airhead from the city with so many big shows coming up. Jackson folded one arm over the other. He also couldn't afford to lose money from his regular customers.

Alexandria walked the horse while Jackson went to the barn office to catch up on billing and veterinary records. After a few minutes, he glanced out the door and saw the bay horse tied in the alley and caught glimpses of her brushing the gelding's back and rear. Alexandria was tall. He saw her shoulders and whole face above the horse's back and noted the soft glow of her heat-moistened skin. She had one of those square faces produced by great-looking cheekbones and a strong chin and jaw. No wonder she did so well in business, he thought as he propped his chin on one hand and continued to watch her. This was his first opportunity to examine Alexandria Payne without having to deal with her at the same time.

She moved to the left side of the horse, and he could see her well through the doorway.

Her rear fit nicely in the Lucky blue jeans that were obviously brand new, and when she brushed across the horse's back and side, the view as she wiggled into her job was pleasant if not impressive. Pulled back in a neat, functional French braid, her blonde hair moved gently across her back. She had a rider's figure: slender, not too busty, and very athletic for a person who spent most of her time in an office. There was no reason she wouldn't do well. He was curious to know why she had only thirty days "to learn everything he knew," but sensed she wouldn't tell him even if he asked.

It didn't matter anyway; in fact, all that mattered was that her check was good. As he tapped his pen on the desk and pondered his good timing, the phone rang.

"Morgan Training Stable," he answered automatically.

"Hey there, young fella. How's come you're not on a horse?"

"Ev." Jackson's face lit up. "Good to hear your hang-dog old voice. Are you going to get up here to see me?"

"Maybe in a couple of weeks. I have to deliver horses to Oklahoma City first. I sold that nice little Doc Bar mare to a high school girl and want to get her settled in right."

"Sounds like you're busy as usual. I just finished a lesson," Jackson said.

"I thought you weren't giving lessons, just training," Everett said quietly.

Jackson drew in a deep breath, leaned back in his chair, and hoped he could avoid the truth. "Well, this one kind of intrigues me. She's hell-bent on learning to cut."

"She, huh. I bet she's pretty as a heifer in a flower bed and has a pretty-please smile."

"I haven't noticed either one," Jackson lied.

"Uh-huh." A long silence followed. "Well, I guess you're old enough to know what you can handle."

"Stop playing father, Ev," he said as Alexandria stepped into the open doorway. She leaned on the jamb, as alluring a picture as Jackson had ever seen, and smiled. "I do know what I'm doing," he said, eyeing her carefully.

"Guess old habits die hard, Jackson; you know you're like a son to me. Ya need anything?"

"Nope. Just looking forward to your visit. We'll get a good game of dominoes going."

"Well, all right. See you at the end of the month."

Jackson hung up and arranged the paperwork and pens on the desk before saying anything. "All your chores done?"

"Of course," she answered.

"Hungry?"

"I thought meals weren't included."

"Ordinarily they're not, but I'm going to eat and I thought you might be hungry too. Besides, for ten thousand, I'll throw in meals."

Alexandria chose to ignore his jab and replied, "I could eat a horse."

He stood, sobered, serious. "Not around here." He moved toward the door. "Peanut butter and jelly is on the menu today."

Alexandria's involuntary shudder brought a smile to his face. She swallowed and he suspected she was swallowing her high-priced tastes in dreaded anticipation of peanut butter.

Once inside the mobile home on the hill, Alexandria immediately went to the bathroom and washed up. Despite the small, cramped quarters, it was heavenly to wash the mud and sludge off her face and hands. There was no washrag available and nothing but Lava soap, so she was forced to stick her face in the sink and splash plain water all over until she felt revived and almost fresh. She grabbed a towel from the rack and buried her face in it.

"What are you doing in there?" Jackson called out from the kitchen. "You haven't fallen in, have you?"

Alexandria opened the door and stepped out, feeling better, but still not entirely clean. "I can see I should have brought my own linens. That towel is…" She rethought the direction she was headed. "Well, I don't want to dirty your *only* towel."

He rolled his eyes. "There are lots more in the closet between the sink and shower, and I have a wonderful, new-fangled thing called a washing machine."

She smiled politely. "Yes, well, be that as it may, I'm sure it will be better if I bring my own."

Earlier, when she had hurriedly thrown her bags in Jackson's bedroom, she hadn't had the chance to look around much. Now she seated herself at the small breakfast bar in the kitchen while he busied himself with lunch and casually examined her home for the next twenty-nine and a half days. All the walls were paneled in that cheap faux wood that mobile homes were famous for, but here and there a nice, framed western print broke the monotony. The kitchen was plain, with no decorations other than a set of hideous sunflower canisters and a small stoneware crock that held utensils. The fact that the sink was immaculate and there wasn't a trace of dirt anywhere except on the floor was impressive for a bachelor, she thought.

Behind her lay the dining room, which sported a reproduction oak pedestal table and four chairs. On the outside wall was a sideboard, obviously an antique, that was topped with a lace doily that looked completely out of place in a residence that indicated no other sign of a feminine touch. Beyond the dining room was the living room. Native American rugs were strategically placed as throws to hide slightly worn furniture.

Alexandria settled back in the bar chair, satisfied she'd seen worse places to live. Besides, she told herself, it was only a month, and for a deal the size of COMJET, she could put up with anything for thirty days.

"Want a soda or lemonade?" Jackson asked as he dug in the refrigerator.

"Is the lemonade fresh?" she asked.

He picked up a cardboard can and read from the label. "Fresh made from frozen concentrate. Yup, it's fresh." He turned the label so she could see it and smiled.

"I'll have a soda, please," she returned with an overly polite tone.

"Suit yourself," he said as he reached back into the refrigerator. "Me, I don't like all that sugar and chemical additives, and I'm sure it's been bottled longer than this lemonade has been frozen, but who am I to tell you how to eat?" He ceremoniously set a can of soda in front of her.

Alexandria looked at the can without touching it. "I'd like a glass, please."

Jackson was now absorbed in building his peanut butter and jelly masterpieces. "Left-hand cupboard to the right of the fridge."

She sighed and got up. Perhaps she'd underestimated how tedious the next month would be.

After lunch they returned to the arena and Jackson mounted her on an older gray mare. "This is Hattie, the babysitter," he said, trying to hide a smirk as he adjusted Alexandria's left stirrup. "She knows more than you and me put together. You'll be riding her until you have a good grasp of what you're supposed to be doing up there."

He grabbed her ankle and shoved her foot all the way to the heel of her boot into the stirrup. "I saw you riding on your toe." He looked up, mischief in his eyes. "That's for those sissy English riders you used to hang out with. Cutters put the stirrup home, like this, right in front of your heel. Less chance of your foot coming out when your horse moves fast."

He was about to continue when her cell phone rang. Alexandria took it from her belt and answered. "Payne here." She listened for only a few seconds, then barked instructions. "I told them it had to be done by noon today; they failed to comply, so go with another bid. I don't care what the excuse is."

Jackson walked to the other side and adjusted her right stirrup.

"Well, you'll have to handle this, but don't back down. We can't afford to—"

He jerked her stirrup and the snap of leather made her jump, although Hattie remained steady.

"Call Paul if necessary. I'll check in later."

Jackson growled as she stuck the phone in the leather holder on her belt, "Is that phone gonna bother you while you're riding?"

"Not at all," she said as she urged the horse away.

"We'll see," he said, walking toward his horse. "Trot, then lope Hattie around to warm her up good, and start getting used to riding on the seat of your pants. Sit on your back pockets."

Alexandria shot a compliant smile at him as she tipped her hips back.

"Better. Now move into a trot..."

She had almost made it around the small arena when her phone rang again. It was Paul.

"What's wrong with your voice?" he said impatiently.

"I'm loosening up by trotting," she said, totally aware that Jackson was listening and rolling his eyes.

"I beg your pardon?" Alexandria could imagine Paul's puzzled expression.

"Never mind, Paul; did Hesperia talk to you about—"

"Yes, that's why I'm calling; you know very well we can't go with the second bid."

"Of course I know; I just wanted them to realize how serious we are, that we mean business. Surely you knew…"

"Reverse," Jackson ordered.

"You can talk with them," she continued, "but don't allow them to bully us."

"Come on, Miss Payne. A little more focus on the horse will work out better. I thought you were in a hurry to learn."

"I'll call you back later." She flipped the phone shut and replaced it on her belt. "I am really good at multi-tasking, Mr. Morgan," she said as she trotted a perfect half circle and reversed direction. Her phone rang three more times over the course of the next hour. Each time Jackson gritted his teeth and became grouchier.

"Stop. This isn't going to work," he said, marching to her as she halted after the phone rang again.

"What are you talking about? I thought I used my legs well on the last couple of circles."

"It's not your legs; it's that infernal cell phone." He slipped it from her belt and threw it over the arena fence where it tumbled down the hillside and was lost in tall grass and bushes.

"What do you think you're doing?"

"I'm putting your mind where it should be. On the horse and on what I tell you."

Alexandria glared.

"Now that we've wasted most of the day with you talking on the phone like a teenager in heat…"

She stepped off Hattie and stomped toward him. "Most teenagers aren't responsible for a multi-million-dollar company, and most teenagers don't have hundreds of people who rely upon them for their salary."

Jackson forced a smile. "No comment about being in heat, Miss Payne?"

"You're right; this may not work out." Her legs were jelly, her back ached, her calves were raw, and she was furious because no matter how she tried to keep things business-as-usual, he could turn her thoughts any way he wanted. "You and I may not be compatible."

He tipped his head and raised one brow in thought. She hoped he wasn't going to call her bluff. Alexandria was certain he needed money, and she was certain she didn't have the time to find another trainer.

"Look," he said after a long pause. "If you get rid of that phone, this will work. You just can't concentrate a bit at a time. Everything between you and the horse has to flow, and every interruption will keep you from feeling or knowing something."

Make him think he's winning, she thought. "OK. No phone while I'm riding, but on the ground, you can't complain."

"Deal. Now get back on and let's finish up."

He put her right back on the fence at a trot and explained a rollback as a quick reverse with no stop. Over and over, he'd told her to sit back, but the first time she tried to execute the rollback, Hattie turned out from under her with surprising speed; Alexandria felt herself heading for the ground, shoulder first.

She hit hard and when she sat up, Jackson hadn't moved from the middle of the arena. Hattie stood staring at her as if to say, "What happened to you?" Alexandria knew she had a fair amount of arena dirt on her shirt and inside of it. Her cell phone rang from its resting place outside the arena in the grass.

Jackson shook his head and stomped toward her. "Why don't we call it quits for today?"

She struggled to her feet. "I can—"

"No. We're done for today." He stopped. "Your legs need a break. You'll likely be stiff as a board tomorrow anyway. Cool Hattie off and put her up while I get started feeding. Oh, yeah, go find your phone when you're done."

He turned and walked toward the gate. Hattie nuzzled her. Alexandria bit back any comment and started walking the mare.

There was more to cutting than she'd thought, and there certainly was more to Jackson Morgan than she'd thought.

Jackson was frustrated as he busied himself with getting the feed buckets set up for the barn. He must have been crazy to agree to this idiotic plan. There had to be another way to get the eighty-five hundred dollars he needed. After a whole month of Alexandria Payne, he might be ready for the lunatic asylum. He'd never met a woman who could irritate him quite as quickly as she did. It was obvious she thought money was the answer to everything and that she also thought he was for sale.

He loaded a bale of hay on the four-wheeler and drove toward the pasture to feed a small pen of calves. If he succeeded in teaching her it would be a miracle—so why did he agree? Because of the eighty-five hundred dollars he owed, *that's why,* he reminded himself. Because he was not going to owe any man, woman, child, or organization, that's why. He opened the gate and threw flakes of hay with a vengeance.

Done, he sat down and listened to the calves milling around him, munching as they moved. He prided himself on being a practical man, and the practical thing to do was to cowboy up and fulfill his part of the bargain.

How bad could it get in a month? What kind of a man was he if he let one little woman get to him? Ev always said he was more hermit than social butterfly, but again, she was only one woman.

He fired up the four-wheeler and rode back to the barn with a new resolve and new patience. *Treat her like a stubborn horse, that's all. Simple.*

As soon as Jackson saw Alexandria standing in the barn, he remembered why it wasn't going to be so simple. Hattie's mane and tail were brushed, there was a huge pile of hair on the ground, and the mare had her ears pinned back like she was running out of patience.

"What are you doing?"

"I can't believe that long tail had so many rats and snarls. We always braided manes and tails to keep them from getting pulled out," she said. "Don't you have tail bags?"

Jackson prayed for strength. "In the tack room, in the last cabinet."

She came out directly with a bag and folded Hattie's tail inside it.

"Thanks for the tail job, but cutters like long manes and tails. The more often you brush them out, the more hair gets pulled out, and the shorter they are."

She looked at him as if he was crazy.

He *knew* she was crazy.

Hattie was tired of them both and wanted to eat.

"OK. Put her in her stall and we'll call it a night." Jackson went to the feed room and shut the door. When he turned around, he saw the halter, the brushes, and the pile of horsehair on the floor. Alexandria was heading for the house.

"Wait a minute. Who's going to put this stuff away?"

She turned to him, a mildly surprised look on her face. "Juan?"

"No. Juan does ranch chores, but he doesn't go around picking up after you or anyone."

She hesitated, then smiled and walked back to the barn. She picked up everything while Jackson watched and then stopped before him.

"Is that all right, Mr. Morgan?"

"That's fine," he said, thinking he'd won another round.

"Good, I'm starved. I hope dinner is ready."

"It will be as soon as I get it out of the can."

Alexandria's smile weakened. "Can?"

"Yup." Jackson mimicked a hillbilly twang. "An' then after dinner, we'll watch home movies."

"Oh, as nice as that sounds, I think I'll pass," she said politely. "I'll just order a pizza or something. I have to shower and call the office and—" Alexandria stumbled as she went from cement barn floor to the gravel outside.

Jackson was close enough to catch her. His hands were strong at her waist. Alexandria felt ever-so-slightly dizzied. She told herself it was fatigue, but somewhere deep inside her, she was afraid it had more to do with Jackson Morgan than with his teaching techniques.

"How long did you say it's been since you rode?" He turned her in his arms and pulled her close at the same time he stood her up.

"Girl Scouts," she said weakly, the truth leaking out.

"You're joking," he said merrily, holding her away. "You haven't ridden since you were a Girl Scout?"

Alexandria pushed him away, angry with herself. "I rode every day as a Girl Scout and received several awards. And I'm fine."

"Hesperia said—"

"I've made it through the first day, and I'll be ready to start at five thirty tomorrow if you want to. In fact, I'll take care of breakfast while you feed."

Jackson smiled as he turned back and pulled the tack room door closed. "Meals weren't included in your deal. Besides, I thought you told me earlier that you never had more than a cup of coffee for breakfast."

She held her chin high. "I usually spend the majority of my time with intellectual exercise, not manual labor." Alexandria jerked the saddle off the horse's broad back and staggered carrying it to the tack room. "I think I'm going to need more than coffee to keep up with you, Mr. Morgan."

"Jackson, Miss Payne, and that's the first reasonable thing you've said."

Jackson insisted she eat with him, and when she found out that the local pizza establishment wouldn't deliver so far out of town, she had no choice but to accept. She showered and was pleasantly surprised to find a simple but adequate meal of barbequed steak, potatoes, and salad. He was very clear that she was not to expect such luxuries on a consistent basis, but Alexandria had developed a plan.

She went to *her* room after the meal and was in the middle of making phone calls when Jackson knocked on the door.

"Movie time," he announced.

"Oh no," she said as she opened the door, too quickly. "I'm beat. I'm going to go—"

Jackson took her by the arm and drew her into the living room where he sat her on the couch. "Just a little while. I want to show you something." He slipped a video cassette into the player and Alexandria prepared to sit just long enough to be polite before she excused herself.

Jackson settled near her with the remote control, totally unaware that his leg brushed against hers, totally unaware that she was miffed that he was unaware. Alexandria wiggled back to relax in the comfortable leather couch, expecting the torture of tedious home movies. The first voice she heard was a lazy drawl that introduced the cutting classes at the World Championship Quarter Horse Show in Texas.

She was relieved.

He was intent.

"Watch this horse," he said as he leaned forward. "See how he gets down low, moves like a cat, and works a cow like he means it. You want a horse like this who'll take control of the cow."

As Alexandria focused on the small screen, she had to admit it was exciting to watch the horse move, especially now that she had some idea of how hard it was to ride the animal in action. Slowly she let herself be drawn into Jackson Morgan's world of high-money cutting horses.

"You can learn something from watching every go. See the man working now? He's an amateur, but has won the World three times. He's got a feel for it most pro trainers don't have."

"Who is he?" Alexandria asked, intrigued.

"Covington."

At once she was interested. "James Covington?"

"Yes, Everett to all his friends." He leaned further forward on the couch, wrapped up in what was on the television. "He gets a hundred percent from every horse I've ever seen him ride, and you need to understand the why before you understand the how."

She nodded. Truer words were never spoken. From that moment on, Alexandria scrutinized the lean older man in the picture. For another hour and a half, they watched horse after horse try to win the coveted World Champion title. None, however, was as impressive to Alexandria as Everett James Covington.

Time was short; she regained her focus. She couldn't afford to be tired; she couldn't afford to be swayed by a grouchy cowboy. There was a lot to learn in only thirty days. Every start, every stop, every turn had to be poetry, written as flawlessly as Covington's performance had been. But that was only an intermediate goal. More important than mere poetry, James Covington was the missing piece to the COMJET puzzle. He was the reason she was in the middle of nowhere, slaving in the dirt like a pauper, tired beyond words, and taking orders from an arrogant cowboy.

CHAPTER 3

Jackson slammed the door to his former bedroom. Alexandria wasn't sleeping like he'd expected her to be, but it was nine o'clock, and she wasn't ready to ride either.

The sound of Booger barking and a car sliding to a halt in the gravel driveway drew him to the front door. He crossed his arms and tapped his toe as Alexandria entered.

"Latte?"

She held a paper cup in both hands with a folder of papers pinned under her arm and smiled as if she had the world by the tail.

"Where have you been? The horses have been fed and are saddled, ready to go before it gets too hot."

"Well," she said as she held out a cup, "you never really said what time we were going to begin today, and I had to fax a couple of things. Do you know there's only one place in Ione that will fax? I was afraid I was going to have to drive all the way back to Sacramento."

"If I thought you were going to be conducting business half the time, I never would have agreed to this deal."

She looked directly at him. "I'm guessing you're angry?"

"Yes." He stomped to her. "I don't have the time to waste sitting around, waiting for you to show up. I don't have the time to teach you if you aren't going to give this your full attention, and I damn sure don't have time to clean up after you in the bathroom or anywhere else. What were you doing in there? There's water everywhere, towels on the floor, and it smells like a French whorehouse. You don't need perfume to ride a horse."

Alexandria stood silent for a moment. "I was under the impression I'd paid for room and board."

"Guess we should have drawn up a business contract since you seem to be misinformed. I'm not your maid."

"Of course not." She sipped her latte. "Clearly you wouldn't know the difference between Givenchy and Bob Mackie without reading the label."

Jackson had no idea what she was talking about. "If you want to ride, be ready in ten minutes; otherwise we'll call off this whole ridiculous thing, Blondie."

"Do...not...call me *Blondie.*"

He smiled. Small battles were suddenly very important to him.

"My name is Alexandria," she said with an air of a small child whose best friend had just called her a name. "And I will be ready to ride."

She spun on her heel and walked to *her* bedroom. Inside, she changed to her jeans and boots, made one quick call, and then went to the barn to find Jackson waiting.

The morning ride was no different than yesterday's, except more intense. Alexandria's whole body was stiff and sore, and at eleven forty-five, when she climbed off the horse, she could barely stand.

Jackson's back was turned as she limped to the hitching rail, tied her horse, and looked at her watch. Every time he looked her way, she stood taller, held her chin up, and forced a smile.

When Jackson disappeared around the corner, Alexandria tapped her toe and checked her watch again. She took her phone from her pocket and punched in only two numbers before a young man sauntered into the barn from the other side.

"Are you Mark?" she asked impatiently as she snapped the cell phone closed.

"Yeah, I—"

"You're late, that's what."

The teen stopped and sobered. "They didn't tell me what time I had to be here."

"Well, if you want to continue as my groom, you'll have to be a lot more prompt."

"Your groom?" Jackson stepped into sight. "We don't have grooms here. We do our own work, for reasons I've already covered, Miss Payne."

Alexandria felt her blood pressure rise. "*We* most certainly can hire a groom and still reap all the benefits of sweating like a pig."

Jackson stepped close and glared at Alexandria. "Pigs don't sweat. You may have been pampered and spoiled wherever it is you live, but you are here now, and if you really want to get as good as you say you do, *I* say no grooms." He slowly turned to Mark, who stood looking like a deer in the headlights. "Miss Payne won't be needing you after all. I'm sure she will pay you handsomely for your time." He glanced back to her. "Isn't that right, Miss Payne?"

Alexandria tossed her best "in your dreams" scowl at Jackson, but he didn't budge.

"All right," she said finally, spitting the words out like bullets. "Here." She dragged two twenty-dollar bills from her pocket and gave them to the teen.

Mark knew when to make his move, and as soon as he had the money in hand, he backed away nervously. "Thanks, appreciate it. See ya later."

The standoff ended when Jackson said very politely, "Unsaddle and put your horse up, please."

The first three days sped by like a shooting star. Despite her crazed mentor, Alexandria willed herself to focus on her mission and get through the month as quickly as possible. The burning in her overtaxed legs gradually subsided, and little by little she regained full range of motion in her lower back so she could move normally. She couldn't remember ever being so stiff and sore, even after her personal trainer put her through a rigorous training schedule, but she wouldn't have admitted it if she had been threatened with death, especially not to Jackson.

Life had settled into a quite comfortable routine with them both rising at five thirty. Alexandria thought she would hate the early hour, but the first time she rose and saw the pastel hues of the sun peeking over the hills, she decided there were benefits to rising at an early hour that she hadn't ever considered. They tried alternating the morning chores, but after two-inch-thick pancakes that were burnt on one side and raw on the other, they agreed it was less frustrating for them both if Jackson cooked. Alexandria actually looked forward to his meals, since Jackson Morgan turned out to be a more than passable chef. Not gourmet, by any means, she reminded him at every chance, but practical, filling, and tasty.

She fed the horses since she seemed to be able to handle the preparation of a flake of hay and a pound of rice bran more competently than eggs and bacon.

After the morning meal, they saddled up. Jackson rode the horses he had in training at the same time he tutored her. Sometimes the lesson was slow and tedious, with turning, stopping, and moving in circles until Alexandria thought she'd go mad. The words *flexion*, *collection*, *action*, *arc*, *timing*, and *serpentine* rattled around in her brain even at night when she tried to sleep. Other times they worked fast, so fast that Alexandria felt like she'd been through a hurricane and back. It fascinated her that a horse could move so quickly and be so smooth, but what truly fascinated her was Jackson.

At times he told her to watch him to illustrate a point or to demonstrate a movement, but it wasn't long before Alexandria found herself sneaking every opportunity to catch a secret glimpse of him working.

Jackson was like a centaur—half man, half horse. He was never left behind, he was never too far forward, and he never made riding look difficult, even on less than cooperative horses. She'd been raised to appreciate the finest, and as she watched him complete a ride on a finished horse, she realized she was watching the finest. He had taught her more in three days than she'd thought she'd learn in a month, and he had a feel for horses, a gentle understanding of them that she envied. The feeling she had as he reined to a sliding stop, backed the gelding, and then let him drop his head and blow was the same one she'd had the first time she'd seen him. A sense of peace unlike anything she'd ever known before enveloped her. That peace was accompanied—no, accentuated—by a definite feeling of power.

He was powerful. Alone with a beautiful creature many times his size and strength, yet he was master through kindness and understanding. Even in the short time she'd been with him, it was obvious that he was a kind and generous master who saw to every need in those under his care.

After several hours of hard work, she walked Hattie to cool her out and begrudgingly admitted she was also very much in his charge. Did she view him as her master also? No, Alexandria shook the ridiculous idea from her head. No man had ever mastered her before, and this one, no matter what kind of insane correlation her mind made, was not going to either. She urged Hattie into a faster walk. She was in charge. The same kind of power was hers, if only she didn't forget her goal.

"Let's hit the trail before it gets too hot." Jackson's gruff voice broke the silence of the arena. Several times before, he had taken her out in the hills to "vary the training schedule and relax a little," as he said. Alexandria was certain he meant it for the horses, but it was a wonderful diversion for her too.

Sometimes they stretched out in a long trot to build stamina and wind, and sometimes, like today, they walked leisurely along trails that followed fence lines or creek beds. A new appreciation for golden, rolling California hills grew, the same way Alexandria had grown to appreciate sunrise. Moving along a narrow, tree-lined trail, a well-bred and beautifully trained horse under her, the sun warming her back, and the sound of nature all around made her feel harmonious and whole.

"Do you ever think about all the thousands of creatures that have traveled over these hills?" she asked as they followed a narrow cattle trail to an old creek bed.

"Nope. I pretty much stick to right now," he answered, slowing his impatient horse as it started up a small incline. "Is that what you've been doing instead of talking like usual?"

Alexandria bristled, saw his "gotcha" smile, then fell back into her newfound state of well-being. "I suppose so. You know there were grizzly bears, elk, and all sorts of flora and fauna here, say, when the Spanish came, and way before that. Feels right to be on horseback, walking along the same paths they used, hearing the same sounds, feeling the heat of the same sun."

"Feeling right is inside you, not around you," he said, holding back so she could cross the creek first. As she rode by, he caught the faint aroma of her perfume mixed with the familiar smell of a horse and saddle leather. Maybe it was the idea of that which was old and familiar melded with something new, rich, and exciting, but Jackson sensed he was riding into uncharted territory.

Some things about her reeked of a hard keeper, like the expensive perfume, the intricate little gold chain around her neck, and the expensive new boots she wore. But then, looking at her, the blonde braid swinging lazily across her shoulders as her horse climbed the bank, or thinking of the way she petted her horse every time it did well, made him think she was as ordinary as he was.

Alexandria's life centered on making things happen. It was what she did and she was comfortable with that, but Jackson realized her sudden connection to things inside and outside herself both intrigued and scared her.

"Inside me," she said, deep in thought, drawing his attention back to their conversation. "I suppose that's true, but I think it's a safe bet to say that you wouldn't feel right in Manhattan, walking shoulder to shoulder with hundreds of people, smelling New York and not honeysuckle."

"Honeysuckle?" he said, still watching her hair. "Where?"

She reined in and pointed to a tree on the creek bank. "There. See the vine tangled in the limbs? That's honeysuckle, and that's the sweet smell you catch on the breeze every so often."

"Well, I'll be darned." He rode to the tree and reached to gather a couple of the tiny ivory horn-shaped blossoms. Turning to her, he sniffed. "They smell a lot like you," he said before thinking, his voice softening.

"One of my favorite fragrances," she said, feeling a bit desperate to be strong. What resulted was more spunk than necessary as she jumped the mare up beside him. "My mother had honeysuckle in the backyard. Daddy said she planted it just before she left us."

"And how old were you?"

"Ten. Daddy married three more times before I was eighteen, but I could always find my mother when I went into her garden. Until wife number three tore up the green garden and replaced it with little rocks and sand in an oriental design."

Jackson plucked a stem with several blossoms, hesitated, then held it out to Alexandria. She knew he was offering, but what scared her was she wasn't sure *what* he was offering. When her fingertips brushed his hand, the look in his eyes, the slight delay before he released the twig, all struck her with a feeling that something more than honeysuckle was passing between them.

She brought the small flowers to her nose and closed her eyes, the fragrance taking her home, taking her to a time when she was alone and desperate for love.

When she opened her eyes, he was watching. He was so quiet, so confident that for the first time in her life, Alexandria was totally unnerved by a man's gaze. Things fluttered somewhere deep in her belly that shouldn't have, and she forced herself to breathe.

He was getting inside her, just as surely as the morning mist and the warm sunshine were. It frightened her in a way that no corporate raider, no tax audit, and no man had ever done before. She tried to look away before he saw through her and realized her weakness, but couldn't.

"Something wrong?"

"No," she answered much too quickly. It was a lie. It sounded good, but Alexandria knew a little bit of her was too aware of how the handsome, sexy cowboy smiled, and was much too impressed with his gentle touch.

She had to be very careful, she reminded herself. She couldn't afford to lose focus now.

"We'd better keep moving. I want to work on turns after lunch." Her hands shook as she picked up and moved her horse away from Jackson, down the road.

"You're taking over as boss man?" he called out after her.

She turned and propped one hand on the horse's fat rump. "We've stopped to smell the daisies. Now don't you think it's time to get back to work?"

"Well, I thought you'd forgotten my number." Paul was in one of those petulant moods that Alexandria hated so.

"I've been busy learning from a slave driver of a teacher. The only thing I haven't had to do is muck out stalls, and I wouldn't put it past him to—"

"I don't want a minute-by-minute account. Are you going to be ready by the end of the month as planned?"

"Yes, I'll be ready," she answered, impatience coloring her tone, "but I do think you might be a little more understanding of what I'm going through. You are clean and comfortable every day in an air-conditioned office with cold drinks and hors d'oeuvres." She fluffed the bed pillow and then punched it, relieving only a paltry amount of tension before lying back. "I *will* be ready. Have you received any more information on COMJET?"

"Not really. We have the same commitments predicated upon delivery. I tried to call you several times, but you were naughty and didn't have your phone on, Alexandria. How am I supposed to keep you informed?"

"Paul. I have my hands full with this cowboy trainer. If you want to trade places, just let me know."

"Ugh. No. I don't think I could handle, literally or mentally, horse manure. You're doing fine, and I imagine you'll have buns of steel when I see you next."

His personal reference to her anatomy didn't set well, but Alexandria chose to ignore it. "You just keep your end up, and as usual, I will handle the dirty work. But listen, I almost forgot that I have good news. Jackson knows Covington, which isn't so surprising considering they're both world-class cutters. I don't want anyone getting suspicious of me being here, since I've come from nowhere, and cutters are a tightly knit group like a family. Do what you can to drop my name in the right places so Covington won't suspect me."

"Will do. How do you plan to arrange an introduction?"

"As I said, Jackson knows him. He'll be my intro, and since we're beginning to travel, I think it'll only be a matter of time until we run into our golden goose."

"We don't *have* a lot of time, Alexandria," he warned in a father-to-child tone.

"I understand that. I'm moving as fast as I can."

"Oh yes, well, kiss, kiss," he sighed. "Got to go, I have another call. Talk to you soon."

He broke the connection and Alexandria reclined in Jackson's bed. She sensed victory, and normally nothing interfered with the smell of success, but this time, her mind wandered. She saw Jackson's soft brown eyes as he handed her the honeysuckle twig and heard his gravelly voice calling for collection and extension. Setting the cell phone on the nightstand, she pulled the covers up and slid down between the sheets. The smell of him lingered all around her. She sat up, punched the pillow again, and threw herself back down.

It had been a mistake to take his bed. Even when she didn't want him, he was here, all around her. From his clothes in the closet to his Western art on the walls to his good felt hats hung carefully by the door, there was no way to escape him.

From the beginning, being around him had encouraged all the wrong things. He smoothed the edge she needed to be sharp and strong and dulled her competitive senses. Although whatever Jackson Morgan gave to her felt good, she told herself it was only temporary, a moment that, like those pleasant rides, would be gone in a month when she returned to the real world. A dog-eat-dog world where she couldn't afford to let her guard down.

It was as simple as he was; the man was dangerous to her well-being and she knew it. She also knew she had no choice but to stick it out until she had what she needed. She was going to have to "cowboy up," as Jackson said again and again, and overcome this childish infatuation with a dreamy modern day warrior.

The next morning, Alexandria woke fresh, determined to deal with Jackson from a new perspective. Her goal was COMJET. Jackson Morgan was an attractive means to get to Covington, but nothing more than that. The next step toward her goal was the winning of a shipping business.

It was obvious that Jackson knew something was different just by the way he acted when she walked into the kitchen after feeding. She went directly to the coffeepot, poured herself a cup, then sat down and waited as if she were ready to be served.

He cocked one brow as he stirred the scrambled eggs. "No problems feeding?"

"Of course not." She sipped from the steaming cup, ignoring his attempts to draw her into conversation. "It's not a difficult job. What are we going to work on today?"

"From the sound of it, we need to challenge you a little, Miss Payne."

"Please, I think it's time you called me Alexandria."

Jackson set out a plate of eggs and toast before he sat down. "All right…Alexandria." He mimicked her perfectly polite, perfectly proper tone, which from him sounded haughty, and her resolve wavered for a fraction of a second. He started eating and she followed suit. Together they ate in silence; "pass the salt and pepper" was as far as conversation went, and each was more than anxious to finish and escape the confinements of the kitchen.

"Well." He pushed away from the table and stood slowly after a stiff, much too formal breakfast. "I'm going to go start saddling up. Come on down when you've cleaned up the kitchen and we'll get started."

Hiding behind her coffee cup, Alexandria watched him leave. Affirming her goals and focusing on the critical issues didn't lend that usual feeling of satisfaction, especially when Jackson left her alone. She knew he was confused by her sudden return to her business-as-usual mode, and to be honest, she was a bit confused herself at why it didn't make her feel more confident.

Why was it important to her that he not walk out shaking his head? Manipulation was a familiar part of everything she did. That was why she was so successful. But the longer she was with Jackson, the more out of control she felt. Her courage was like water swirling down the drain, hard to hold on to and even harder to gauge.

Closing her mind to the possibility that her courage was failing, she rose from the table, gathered and washed the dishes, and left the kitchen. She'd wasted enough time thinking that Jackson would surely wonder where she was. Back in her room, she purposely took her time brushing her teeth. Then, a short, quick call to Paul on the way to the barn confirmed her priorities, and within steps, she congratulated herself on being able to handle Paul, business, *and* Jackson Morgan.

When she finally appeared at the barn, she found him in back, brushing a black horse that was obviously past its prime. His muzzle was sprinkled with gray and his back was gently swayed. Jackson heard her and turned, his nod inviting her closer.

"This is Joker, the old man of the ranch."

"Exactly how old is he?" she asked, caressing his sunken brow.

"At least twenty-eight, but"—he held his hand over the gelding's ears—"don't tell him that. He still thinks he's a colt."

Alexandria ran her hand along the silken neck and over the long mane. "You don't show him, do you?"

"No." There was love in Jackson's tone and in his touch. "He was my first horse. The first time I did really well in a class, this horse did it for me, and he took me to a Junior National Championship. He's retired now and he'll be here until he dies."

Alexandria was a bit surprised to find such compassion in a man whose tools of the trade were horses. The strength of a bond, simple trust between man and horse, suddenly hit her and she was both touched and envious as the old horse nuzzled Jackson for more attention.

Joker's reward was Jackson's gentle rubbing of one ear, then the other. "Well, Joker will keep me here all day, but we have things to do. Let's get going before the heat hits. I hear it's going to be one hundred and five today."

She groaned, knowing full well that heat, even over a hundred, made no difference in the way Jackson Morgan drove himself and her. In minutes, they both started out a long day with a warm-up routine that was normally no problem. Today, however, Alexandria was having trouble being part of *the team.*

She didn't seem to be able to sense what the horse needed, and Jackson wasn't sure if it was because she wasn't trying or because she wasn't concentrating. The end result was a series of rough, on-the-front-end stops, sloppy turns, and egg-shaped circles that were driving him crazy.

"All right." He finally gave up. "Why don't you take a break and come turn back for me? I need to work on that new palomino mare."

Alexandria had seen the mare when she was delivered the day before. Gorgeous, shiny like a copper penny, the horse belonged to a new client and was very green. Alexandria watched Jackson move slowly into the herd, making a shallow cut on one of the cows in the front, and then allowing the rest, one by one, to escape back to the herd until the one he'd selected to work was left. Then he'd stop and settle the mare, giving her a chance to be quiet and relaxed.

As he worked, he detailed to Alexandria what he was doing, what the horse wanted to do, and what he needed the horse to do. "Being young and new at this, she's in a hurry. She wants to charge the cow, go too fast, so I have to keep her a little farther from the herd and teach her to stay back and go slower. People are sometimes like that too." He flashed a smile meant for her after the comment, but never took his eye off the cow or his attention away from the mare he rode.

"This horse needs to understand that she can get as much or more done by relaxing a little. She'll stir up the cows less and end up having the time to think out what she's doing."

Alexandria knew he was talking about her as much as he was talking about the horse, but her renewed cool dictated that she ignore the double meaning. "Would it help to make deep cuts into the herd instead of shallow ones? I mean, will having more cows sift by her teach her to be patient?"

Jackson pulled up and let the cow return to the herd. "Sometimes," he said as he selected another cow, "but it will frustrate her to do that all the time; you have to be aware of how your horse reacts to everything you put in front of her. You never want to bore an animal by doing the same thing all the time. That was part of what was going wrong with you earlier. You didn't feel the horse's frustration."

"I don't know that I'll ever be able to *feel* it as easily as you do."

He rode to her side, patting the palomino mare on the neck. "It is easy when you take your time and think. Go on out and try for that black cow with the white face. She's pretty slow so you'll have plenty of time to figure out where you belong."

Alexandria had no problem separating the black cow from the herd, but on the first cut, she allowed her gelding to get long, ahead of the cow, and was left behind as the cow turned back and loped to the herd.

"Go back and get her," Jackson ordered. "You weren't thinking."

Alexandria tried to do as she was told, but continued to ride long.

"What *are* you thinking about?" Jackson called out. "You're not focused; you're way late."

Irritated by her inability to catch up and angry with herself for making mistakes that she hadn't been making lately, she spurred and punched the gelding up, and lost the cow again.

"Where's your mind?" Jackson said, his voice clearly indicating his disappointment. "Try it again. That horse knows what to do, and you're not letting him work. You're back into this control thing we fought the first day. Let him work."

Alexandria took a deep breath, swallowed a scathing retort, and headed into the herd, choosing a smaller red cow. Forcing herself to concentrate on the cow and her position, she made the first several cuts. Tormented and annoyed, she quickly reminded herself it would only be a matter of time before Covington was putty in her hands.

Immediately, as if the cow knew her mind had turned elsewhere, it ran past her. Irritated, she pulled up and slumped in the saddle.

"No!" Jackson said, his tone punishing her. "Don't ever do that. The horse was still working the cow, and when you pulled him up and let the cow back to the herd, you taught him to quit. It's called a hot quit and costs you five points. You taught him to take the easy way out when it gets a little rough."

Alexandria had had enough of him, the cows, and even herself. "There are good days, Jackson, and bad days." She dismounted. "This has been a bad day, and I'm done."

Jackson dismounted and stood before her. "Hot quit for you too?"

She stopped and glared. "I never quit. I'm not making any progress today, and I know better than to keep making mistakes."

"I still think it's a hot quit."

"I don't care what you think."

"You're paying me a lot of money to tell you what I think."

"Well, today is your day off. I don't want to hear—"

"Hear this. You are the most stubborn, disagreeable woman I've ever met."

"So what's your point? Liking me was never part of the deal."

His eyes grew dark and brilliant. He shook his head, and when he spoke, his voice was low and dangerous. "No, it wasn't part of the deal at all."

"Well, maybe you—"

Jackson smiled as he silenced her by touching a finger to her lips. That maddening flutter deep in her belly hit as soon as she knew his touch was imminent and grew into a blinding sense of radiating heat.

From her lips, his hand stroked her cheek and she swore he'd branded her. The heat grew. Alexandria tried not to lean into his caress.

Jackson stepped closer, cupped her face between his fingers, and pulled her to him. His lips on hers were electric. Strong, possessive, commanding.

The only thing on Alexandria's mind now was Jackson Morgan. The pressure of his mouth backed her against the horse's hot side. A primitive yearning, deeper and more intense than the heat that was already overwhelming, drove Alexandria to the brink. He was like a storm, promising a wild ride, and sure to deliver satisfaction.

CHAPTER 4

Jackson couldn't believe he was kissing her. He didn't know what had come over him, but at this point it didn't matter. Her soft lips and heated response to his touch was what mattered. That, and the fact that she was the most exciting, most stimulating woman he'd ever known. There were all sorts of reasons this shouldn't have happened, but he couldn't think of a single one.

All he could think of was her.

She was fire and honeysuckle; she was smart and strong, and he knew from the moment his lips touched hers that he had to have her.

Slowly he pulled away. His lips had barely left hers when her eyes fluttered open and she stared at him with undisguised hunger. Passion glittered in her blue eyes.

A tiny smile broke out over her face, and he knew she'd enjoyed being kissed as much as he enjoyed kissing her.

"That was…" Her voice broke and she cleared her throat. She slowly shook her head and hesitated, a little too long for his taste, as she searched his face. Then, as if she forced each word, she continued in a hoarse whisper. "As nice as that was…I can't have it happen again."

"Why?" he asked, still close enough to kiss her and still wanting to. "Because you don't have control?"

"No." She flattened herself against the horse to put even a little more distance between them. "Because I don't want you to. I don't want to have an affair, I don't—"

"An affair?" He backed away a little. "I'm not looking for an affair. You may be sleeping in my bed, but that doesn't mean that's the only thing on my mind."

Alexandria dropped her head and licked her lips, trying to buy enough time to tell herself that he didn't have a kiss that turned her inside out from the toes up and that he wasn't everything a normal red-blooded woman hungered for.

He picked her chin up and made her look at him. "I'm not sure what's going on either. All I'm asking is that you stay around long enough for us to find out."

"I have less than a month," she said. "That's not enough. You're part of a summer dream and I realize that. You must know and understand that too."

Each word was precise, sharp, and he knew she intended to set him in his place, but Jackson also knew he had to allow Alexandria a little freedom both on the horse and off. Despite her worldly ways and her bravado, he suspected she was like a bristly colt that needed to trust a rider before he got on and rode.

"OK. You get a five-point deduction for a hot quit, and we'll start over after lunch." He turned and walked away. He wasn't going to coddle, and he sure as hell wasn't going to beg. It was obvious she needed something besides stiff corporate meetings and CEOs. There was a softer side to her. A side that let her feel and enjoy the miracle of Mother Nature's gift to cowy horses. A side of her that let her fall in love with honeysuckle and the way a horse nuzzled just to be touched.

The rest of the day, she worked harder than ever for him, no matter what he asked of her, no matter how hard he pushed. She was focused, determined, and nearly perfect.

It wasn't easy for Jackson to ignore the memories of the heated kiss, and by the time he crawled into his couch bed, he felt like screaming. He wasn't the screaming type, but Alexandria's ability to shut down could have been listed as one of the wonders of the world.

Since the stolen kiss he'd watched her pretend nothing had happened when they both knew better. Try as he might, Alexandria was hard to reckon with. She was one of the most savvy women he'd ever seen, and it annoyed him to see her sail through life and yet fail when it came to a personal relationship.

Once or twice in the last two days, there'd been a moment charged with electricity when, by pure coincidence, his hand had touched hers, or brushed her leg, or settled on her shoulder. Coolly, but without hesitation, Alexandria had moved away, as if the smallest sign of warmth was too much to bear. Jackson longed to take her in his arms again and explore the passion he'd seen so briefly in her eyes and felt in her kiss, but the horseman in him knew she was a lot like a skittish colt. It was vital to her spirit that he be patient and go slowly. Exactly as he would have done with that colt, he was willing to wait in expectation of the grand things the future might hold.

Just take it one day at a time. He planned his strategy to win Alexandria's heart at the same time he planned her learning schedule. The local cutting club had a practice every Friday night in which Jackson usually participated, and he figured Alexandria was ready to go and help out. Most cutters brought their own turn-back help, riders who hung out on the edge of the herd and kept the herd together while the cutter worked, but there were always some who needed herd help from other cutters. Alexandria wasn't ready to cut per se, but she was ready to help and could turn back while he worked clients' horses.

That evening, the fiery red sun hung low in the sky and cast a serene glow across the hills, and Alexandria found driving along the narrow back roads of California's gold country amazing on several fronts. She couldn't imagine a world more different from skyscrapers, freeways, and computers, and it seemed more dreamlike than ever when she remembered that a month ago, she couldn't have imagined herself in this truck, with this man, in this beautiful country, going to a cutting.

Jackson was next to her in the cab of the dually pickup, and at the moment his concentration was on negotiating the narrow, winding road with the truck and gooseneck trailer. Instead of the various T-shirts he'd worn ever since she'd come, he now wore a crisp, long-sleeved western shirt with tiny maroon and navy checks that made his broad shoulders and wide chest more obvious than ever. His strong, muscled hands moving on the steering wheel were a constant reminder of how good it felt when he held her and how incredibly electric his lips on hers had been.

Since the kiss, she'd been hard pressed to think of much else. As often as she'd told herself that, for her own good, she had to ignore the feelings, they returned and haunted every minute of her days and especially her nights.

She looked out the window and saw nothing but Jackson's reflection in her window. Every nerve in her body was aware of how close he was and that they were alone. Pretending to admire the scenery beyond him, she sneaked another look at the handsome, virile man. The air-conditioned cab was cool, but a warm glow surrounded her as she thought of how much more complicated and powerful he was than she first thought. He was no ordinary cowboy, and he certainly was not an easy mark.

Jackson flicked the turn signal on, and Alexandria's observant nature immediately assessed her surroundings. The drive they turned on was lined with tall poplar trees and a white vinyl board fence. Ahead, sprawled across a small knoll, was a magnificent house that Alexandria knew must have approached ten thousand square feet. There was a four-car garage, the fourth space being tall enough to accommodate a motor home; off to the side there was an equally magnificent barn and indoor arena.

"Nice place," she commented as they drove in and parked next to several other large truck and trailer rigs.

"Trisha doesn't do things halfway," Jackson answered as he turned off the engine. "She has a housekeeper and a cook and they all live here." He glanced toward the house. "Can you tell?"

Alexandria noted a hint of disapproval in his tone. "You don't think it's right to have a nice house?" she teased, thinking of her father's estate in Newport Beach.

"None of my business," he said stoically as he got out and closed the door.

Alexandria's curiosity was piqued by his tone. "Then what?" She followed him to the trailer where they began unloading horses. "What is it about this place that—"

"Nothing." He tied one horse to the trailer and began brushing. "Trisha is a very nice person; I just can't take her collector attitude."

"Collector attitude?" Alexandria asked as she brushed Hattie.

"Everything she sees has to be hers if she doesn't have something better, that's all. She collects things even if she doesn't want or need them."

"I see. What if she does want something? Then it's all right?" She worked her finger through Hattie's mane and peered over the sleek neck, still provoking him.

He brushed the horse and eyed Alexandria cautiously, as if he suspected he might be stepping into a carefully plotted trap. "Like I said earlier, it's none of my business. Right now, I need to get two more horses saddled and ready. Finish Hattie and saddle that palomino for me, will you?"

He stepped up into the tack room, ending the conversation. Alexandria quickly saddled Hattie and started on the palomino. By the time Jackson was leading two horses toward the arena, she followed with Hattie and the other mare. As Jackson tied one horse to the fence and turned to mount the second, a stunning, dark-haired woman with a walk any cat would admire came up to him.

"Jackson, darling. So glad to see you." She threw her arms around his neck and planted a quick kiss on one cheek, then a longer, quite possessive one on his lips. "Come see the new filly I bought," she said as she drew back. "She's a Doc Bar baby, and I'm just going to have to find a good trainer to start her." She fluttered long, beautiful lashes at him and leaned seductively against his chest. "Know anybody who is *really good*...at training?"

Alexandria felt heat rise in her face, but immediately rejected the idea she was jealous. "Shall I tie this mare up, Jackson?" she called out, intentionally interrupting his conversation.

He looked back to her, and she swore his expression was one of gratitude. "Yeah, over there by the round pen is good. Alexandria Payne, this is Trisha Wolcott. This is her place."

Trisha walked up to Alexandria and extended her hand. "Nice to meet you—Alicia."

Alexandria smiled, assessing the other woman's qualities as she reached. "Alexandria," she corrected. "Jackson has told me all about you, I—"

"You need to get in and warm up," Jackson broke in with a warning glance, then turned to Trisha. "Where's this new filly? How old..."

Trisha tossed Alexandria a triumphant smile as she took Jackson's arm and pulled him close. They were partially hidden by the horse he led, and whatever they said became unintelligible. Alexandria stood, doing a slow burn. There was so much to dislike about the woman that she didn't know where to start, but probably the kiss was a good place.

Well, what did you expect? He's an attractive man. It's perfectly reasonable and natural that he'd be spoken for or involved, as she was. She tied the palomino and mounted Hattie. Besides, it should be easy now to get back on target and forget everything about him except that he was providing a service.

She began her warm-up by trotting in slow, limbering circles. He was an *employee* and she certainly had no problem staying away from employees. She punched Hattie into a lope, and when the mare jumped ahead, Alexandria reminded herself the worst thing she could do now was to let her emotions run wild. It was so unlike her and so counterproductive.

Loping was relaxing for her. The cadence of the horse's stride and the mare's rhythmic breathing as they both settled into the business of cutting was mesmerizing.

The announcer began calling for riders to sign up for the practice and Alexandria began to wonder where Jackson was. It had been quite some time since he'd disappeared, and it wasn't like him to be late for anything, including a warm-up.

When at last he appeared he was still on Trisha's arm. Alexandria tried to ignore how Trisha smiled at him, then delivered a chaste kiss to his cheek before he mounted and rode off to warm up. Despite her resolve to remain uninvolved and emotionless, Alexandria wondered how many other kisses there'd been that she hadn't seen.

Jackson trotted toward her, and Alexandria immediately busied herself with a flexion exercise intended to soften the horse's neck and jaw. Sober and intent upon the warm-up, he continued past without a word.

He certainly didn't owe her any explanations, and she had no right to expect polite chitchat when he had a job to do. Then why was she gritting her teeth and feeling like she'd just been snubbed?

Suddenly impatient, she jabbed a spur into Hattie who leaped forward and threw her head up, negating all the work she'd just done to relax her.

"What was that?" Jackson called out from a short way behind her. "That wasn't smooth or subtle."

She turned and looked at him as he trotted closer. "Oh yes, I forgot how much you like smooth and subtle," she said more sharply than she'd intended, thinking only of Trisha's smooth and not-so-subtle flirtation.

He reined in near her, a sparkle in his eye. "Am I missing something?"

"No." She urged Hattie into a lope without looking his way. "I don't think you're missing anything."

Jackson halted, dropped his reins on the horse's neck, and smiled as he patted the glossy hide. "I swear I'm gonna figure her out." He shook his head, picked up the reins, and moved out at a lope muttering to himself, "And when I do, it's gonna be good."

The evening went along well, with Jackson working several times and Alexandria turning back for him. Once, she got so involved with watching him and the beauty of a well-trained team that she forgot her job and lost the cow when it came to her in her corner. But he took it well and used it as a learning experience. Everybody there was friendly, although it was understood that each one of them was out to win, something Alexandria understood very well. Waiting on the sidelines had never been her strong suit. She could hardly wait to get in the arena and cut a cow instead of merely sitting in the corner helping.

Practice was almost over when Trisha came to Jackson and Alexandria as they sat to the side on their horses.

"I need turn back help, Alexandria," she said as she smiled at Jackson and ran her fingers through her pixie hair. "Feel up to it?"

Jackson knew Trisha was trouble and was about to reply when Alexandria answered instead. "Sure." Picking up her reins, Alexandria eased Hattie out.

Behind her Jackson's soft growl echoed. "Take your time, you'll have no problem."

When she had Hattie settled in the corner spot, Alexandria did just as Jackson taught her. She concentrated on the cow as if she were working it and when it came close, she merely stood her ground to send it back to Trisha. Almost all the way through Trisha's two-minute run, the cow stalled in front of Hattie and then faked a turn to the left and blasted right past her.

"You did that on purpose," Trisha wailed. "I had a good go working and *you* let my cow out."

Alexandria was momentarily at a loss for words. She'd been doing everything by the book and suddenly, faster than she'd ever thought possible, the cow was gone and everything was out of control. But it had never occurred to her to do it on purpose.

"That's the last time you'll ever turn back for me. Jackson said you were green, and I used you as a favor to him, but"—she shook her head sorrowfully as she rode off—"*that* was the last time."

Alexandria watched the dark-haired woman ride to Jackson, who appeared to commiserate. She'd had enough. She turned Hattie toward the trailer where she unsaddled, brushed, and threw a stable sheet on the mare before Jackson finally came.

"Well, what did you think?" he said, as if Trisha hadn't just cried all over his very willing, very strong, and capable shoulder.

"About the practice or about your friend Trisha?" she answered testily.

"The practice, of course; that was the idea in coming here. You did great except for that one cow. Do you know what happened?" he said more evenly than she thought he would.

"I lost the cow. It was a pretty straightforward mistake on my part."

"Probably. But if you had known the stock better and you had more experience reading cows, you would have expected it. That particular one will do that every time the cutter lets up a little and gives it room, and you could see by her head and watching her eye what she was up to. You have to stick tight to it when you're there. Some people will be pretty honest and tell you about the cows if you ask, but if you can't find out anything, then you have to really keep an eye out for trouble."

She led Hattie into the trailer and tied her. On her way out, she stopped, facing Jackson as he was about to load his horse. "You mean she knew that cow was going to fake it and then get away from me?"

He smiled. "Guaranteed, once you got a little loose in the corner."

"And Trisha could have prevented it?"

He moved past her and tied the horse. "Maybe. You can't always tell, but she's good enough—"

"I see," Alexandria said flatly, recognizing a setup when she saw it. Now, angry with herself for falling into a trap, she left abruptly to get the third and fourth horses. When she returned and handed one lead rope to Jackson, he had a mischievous little grin on his face. She knit her brows and challenged him. "You think this is funny, don't you?"

"Nope. None of my business." He tied the horse and reached for the last lead. "I learned long ago to stay out of the way when ladies have a thing going."

Alexandria crossed her arms and stood by the trailer door. She felt like a child in the midst of a tiff, but as sure as she knew what a hot quit was, Trisha was the one who had fired first. The thing to do was ignore her, not dignify the dirty trick with a response, but for some reason the idea was harder to digest than rubber boots.

She watched Jackson, who acted as if he'd seen or heard nothing all evening. He stepped out of the trailer and latched the door on the horses. He was calm, cool, and definitely enjoying her situation, which tweaked her patience just a little more.

Like the get-away cow, her perfectly controlled and ordered life had suddenly gotten away from her. And the reason was standing in front of her.

Like a handsome shadow, he moved in the moonless night toward the driver's door, while Alexandria, irritated with herself, wondered exactly when she'd swapped her trademark calm, cool perspective with Jackson Morgan for that of a clinging woman. So many things were going through her head right now, not the least of which was the fact that she was engaged. More of a business relationship, but at the moment, Alexandria felt guilty for hiding what she originally deemed personal and none of Jackson's business.

Not yet desperate, but certainly off balance, she wandered toward him and the truck. "Alexandria," she heard him say. "Check the tack room door and make sure it's closed."

Might as well be hired help, she thought as she doubled back. Unconsciously, she twisted the handle to check it, while consciously she checked a nasty impulse to fire back a reply. She then continued to the passenger side of the truck where she got in and slammed the door. If Trisha Wolcott wanted him, she could have him. It was none of her business, and from now on, she was going to treat Trisha just like any other person in the world.

They got home a few minutes before eleven, and it was midnight by the time they had all four horses put up. Both she and Jackson were tired. They fell into bed, and even though a wall separated them, each slept as one, tossing and turning, a powerful yearning destroying all hope of restful slumber.

When the alarm went off at four a.m. on Saturday, Jackson slapped at the clock to shut it off and groaned. The lumpy couch was getting harder and harder to ignore as was the way he felt about his only pupil. He rose and knocked on her door, reminding her they were going to a show in Reno and had to be loaded and gone by five a.m. Both moved automatically and both were too tired to trade shots or parry on any level. Business was the word of the day.

Jackson placed well in several classes while she redeemed herself riding turn back. At the end of a long day, Alexandria was exhausted and much too tired to do anything but what she was told. She dragged herself to bed thinking she'd be glad to get back to the gym where the exercise level was normal.

Sunday, Alexandria slept in and Jackson went alone to see a client in the gold rush town of Auburn. Jackson had trained several horses for the man and his young daughter and now was going to give his opinion on a yearling filly. Monday he had business in Sacramento and left Alexandria with a list of things to practice and do. The next day he was back, and they returned to a rigorous schedule: riding most of the day, studying videos, and reading the rule book to fill any spare moments.

Alexandria was a demanding student, eager to learn and forever asking questions. Keeping her busy both mentally and physically was a challenge Jackson handled better than the challenge of finding the appropriate place for her in his mind. The more tuned she became as a rider, the more tuned he was to her body and the seductive way she had of drawing the best from every horse he put her on, despite her being a green rider. The more savvy she became about cutting horses, the more he realized she had the kind of talent that few riders ever dream of, much less achieve. She was a smart and complicated woman, and it began to weigh heavily upon him that there were a lot of unanswered questions where Alexandria Payne was concerned.

Late in the afternoon on Wednesday, Jackson was riding turn back for her. Slowly the realization came to him that she was working on two different things: one on horseback, riding a belligerent roan mare, and the second, treating him as if he was nothing more than hired help.

She finished with as nice a ride as he'd seen on the lazy mare; he was delighted with her progress and achievement but was having a hard time finding something nice to say when his own frustration level was high and rising. It had been a long day so far, and his patience with himself was wearing thin. The thirty-day time limit was beginning to torment him. Professionally, he saw so much potential in her that needed more time to grow. Personally, he'd made little or no progress with Alexandria, the beautiful, intriguing woman of mystery.

She'd made sure there were no chances for a second kiss, no matter how much Jackson would have liked it. He had to admire her ability to immerse herself totally in the business of learning, but she purposely left no room for anything else, especially him, and it was driving him crazy.

He chose his words carefully. "Something must have clicked for you in the last day or two, Alexandria. That last go was smooth as silk and twice as clean."

"Thanks," she said, a broad smile relating her satisfaction as she dismounted and patted the horse's neck. "It feels better too. I'm reading the cow better, and I can get in position before it's too late."

"Alexandria," Jackson began, stepping closer, hoping he might chip away at the barrier she'd put between them.

"Yes?" She looked directly at him, as if he were nothing more than a stranger on the street.

He stepped back. "Nothing." He was like a schoolboy trying to ask for his first date. "Nothing, except I think you're ready to cut at Rancho Murieta this weekend. You'll get a taste of real competition. What do you think?"

Alexandria watched him for a moment. Her first thought should have been that Covington might be there. But the fact that what he'd said was not what he originally intended had been written all over his face. It hurt just a little bit that he hid his real thoughts from her, and his eyes held a twinge of pain that hurt even more because she knew she was the source.

"What?" she said when she realized Jackson was staring at her.

He took the reins from her, turned his back, and began to loosen the cinch. "After all this work, I'da thought you'd be a little more excited about some real honest-to-goodness competition.

I swear, Alex, I can't figure you out. You run hot and cold like a thunder shower in summer."

He mounted the roan and walked the horse toward the stalls; she knew it was his way of closing the conversation. He was shutting her out. Well, wasn't that what she wanted? Wasn't that what she needed in order to focus on Covington and the COMJET deal?

"Wait a minute," she said, more commanding than she intended. Then her voice softened when she realized what he'd said. "What did you call me?"

"Alex," he called out, his back still to her. "I'm getting tired of dealing with *Alexandria*."

"What do you mean by that?" she said, jogging to catch up.

Jackson stopped. He eyed her carefully as she walked in front and faced him. "I'm tired of saying Alexandria. I want something shorter, something…less formal."

He sighed, and instantly she sensed his frustration.

"Come on. Allow me this one shortcut. City slicker Alexandria wouldn't be standing here, with sweat about to drip from her temples, with dirt on her face and her hair trying to escape that awful braid." *And needing to be kissed.*

She stared long and hard. Again, it wasn't the whole truth and she knew it. She took a deep breath, exhaled, and gazed at her scuffed, dirty boots. "All right." She slowly looked up and found his soft brown eyes fixed upon her. She laughed, a flirtatious sparkle in her eye. "You're right. This is Alex." She held her arms wide for inspection.

Jackson was relieved. She saw his shoulders relax and his tense expression faded.

"I like Alex." The soft timbre of his voice sent her pulse racing, and suddenly Covington was nowhere in her thoughts. It wasn't hard to imagine herself in Jackson's strong arms, and it was even easier to imagine how good his lips would feel… everywhere.

"So do I," she whispered, afraid to admit how much she wanted to be Alex for him. Looking up at him on horseback made her feel small, feminine, and very awkward. Her heart was beating in her throat and she swallowed hard. "And I'd love…to go to Rancho Murieta and cut." *With you.*

"Well, all right," Jackson said. "We'll celebrate your debut tonight. Go ahead and clean up, and I'll take care of chores."

He rode away, leaving Alex alone with Alexandria. Jackson Morgan was not candles, champagne, and roses. He was hard work and success earned by courage and determination. It was the little things that counted with him. She backed toward the mobile home on top of the knoll, unwilling to lose sight of him until the last minute when he disappeared into the dark recesses of the barn. Could she be Alex for him, or was it truly a summer infatuation with a cowboy, an obsession with a fantasy hero who rode like a king and kissed like a man on fire?

As she showered she warred with herself. It was such a small thing, the name, but when he said it, suddenly things were different. She knew she was the same person she'd always been, but she now felt like a book with a new chapter—a chapter on feeling, on being alive. Jackson was the author of *Alex*. She suspected he was waiting for her to do something. The unnerving thing was she had no idea what it was. Learning from him was so much easier than being with him. When it came to goals, she was a master, but when it came to feelings, she was not so adept.

It was important to her that whatever she did now be simple and honest; Jackson wouldn't appreciate anything else. Suddenly an idea came to her. She dressed quickly, scribbled a note about running to town, and was off.

Driving along the rutted road, she was pleased with herself and excited about her plan. In the small town of Ione, she purchased a half-gallon of ice cream, bananas, hot fudge topping, and whipped cream. Even someone as inept in the kitchen as she was could surely put together a tempting fudge sundae.

Driving back, Alexandria rolled the windows down and took the rubber band from her hair. Alex didn't care if her hair was unruly and messed up. Alex needed to feel free and alive. Alex relished the feel of the wind on her cheeks and rush to her soul. The world smelled like oak trees and golden grass. She was farther from the city than she'd ever been.

There was still a half hour of daylight left when she pulled into the drive that led to the mobile home on the hill. Even from a distance she could see a car parked in front of the house. As she rolled closer, she saw it was a sleek black BMW.

Alexandria parked next to the car, gathered her bags, and stepped out. The euphoria of the windy ride vanished, and she cautiously walked across the porch to the open door of the mobile home.

"Of course." Paul's voice was perfect and clear through the screen. "Alexandria is very much her own woman. When she sets her mind on a goal, there's nothing that will stop her, as I'm sure you've noticed."

Alexandria noticed only that there was no answer.

"She was voted American Business Woman of the Year twice in the last five years, and..."

Alexandria pushed through the front door and found Paul chatting amiably with Jackson. Paul was sitting tall with a glass of iced tea, suave as ever, impeccably dressed. Jackson reclined in his chair, jeans still dusty and boots scuffed and worn, a look of polite boredom fixed across his face.

On seeing her, Paul rose. "Darling." He smiled, but Alexandria couldn't help but notice that his smile didn't reach his eyes as Jackson's always did. He approached and kissed her, his lips dry and stiff on hers, then he curled one arm over her shoulders possessively. "I've missed her so very much."

Alexandria couldn't take her eyes off Jackson, who remained seated, watching her. "I see you've met Paul. He's—"

"He's told me all about himself, and you," Jackson said dryly. "Now that you're here," he said as he stood, "I have things left to do at the barn."

Jackson grabbed his hat from the rack by the door and left. The sound of the screen door slapping echoed in her mind and she slid from under Paul's arm. Alexandria went to the kitchen to put away the ice cream. He stood silent, but watched her. She finally turned to face him.

"Have I come at an inopportune time?" he said more prissily than normal as he dusted off the bar stool and seated himself.

"No." She poured herself a glass of tea, then returned the pitcher to the refrigerator. "The way you're looking at me, I get the feeling that you're checking up and I don't appreciate it."

"I just sensed from your phone calls that you might need some cheering. Of course this last week, I heard from you only three times...you can't possibly blame me for worrying about you."

She sipped slowly, taking her time to reply. "It's not like you, Paul."

"And it's not like you to forget where you're going, to lose your direction."

"And who says I have?" She shot a punitive glance at him. "I've always handled things on my own, in my own way. You never complained before." She sipped again, daring him to answer.

He stood and set his glass down. "All I'm saying is that the COMJET pieces are falling into place and I wanted to see if I could help." He wandered close and balanced her chin on his forefinger. "We are a team, Alexandria."

Her name sounded like a curse on his lips, and she felt the need to pull back, but didn't. She stared into his frivolously blue eyes, noting for the first time their lack of compassion. "Yes, we are a team." She turned away to compose herself, then spun back. "We are a devastatingly effective business team, but you have to trust me, Paul. I haven't lost a bit of my direction any more than you have. I am on a mission for APM, and I never fail."

"What a relief to hear that," he said in a monotone. "How about I take you to dinner? There's a quaint little inn at Sloughhouse that has a good reputation in this area. We can discuss what's been going on since you've been gone."

Jackson wanted to punch something, but instead he chose to vent his frustrations while riding. All his life, he'd been able to find a kind of nirvana in the saddle, but tonight, as dusk fell across the golden hills, all he could think of was what a fool he'd been.

Riding in circles only reminded him of how she'd had him wrapped around her little finger, of how he'd turned somersaults to find the key to her, or how much he'd really wanted her to be his. Of all the women he'd ever known, Alex was the first one he couldn't brush off. There had been others with whom he'd spent time, but none who had bridled his soul and reined in his heart like she did.

Jackson heard the BMW leave, and like a spirited horse that searches for freedom, he finally gave up the confines of arena work and headed for the hills. The moon was just big enough to cast an eerie shadow over the countryside, and the massive oaks looked to be gargoyles across the rolling landscape. By now the hot summer air was beginning to give way to the cooler night breeze. After living in a heated rush for two weeks, the evening cool was welcome, and it matched the dull, cold feeling in his soul.

She had been using him. It was his own fault too. She had sent him signal after signal that it wasn't going to work, but he, the optimist, had ignored them all. He had been a fool.

The horse stepped out lightly on the trail and Jackson wished he could disappear into the night. The deal he'd made with Alexandria had two weeks more or less to go, and he wasn't quite sure how he was going to deal with her. It had occurred to him to cancel the deal, but he wasn't a man to give his word lightly. If he lost everything, he still had his honor.

Perhaps it was something Alexandria Payne had overlooked in her strange determination to learn to cut, but nevertheless, it was an ideal he chose to live by; it made it impossible to turn tail and run from her.

He supposed the best thing was to approach it as he would the training of any horse. Stick to business. He'd done it often enough with women like Trisha; he could do it with Alex.

Having reached some conclusion, even though it was not the ideal one, he finally allowed the horse to head for home. When he rode into the barnyard, he noted the lights were off in the house except for the dim glow of the lamp in the living room. Since tomorrow was going to be a full day, Alex probably had gone to bed already and that was good.

He had no desire to see her tonight.

He set about unsaddling and putting up the horse, but just as he closed the stall door, he heard the crunch of tires on the gravel in the driveway. Several seconds later, a car door closed and he heard the engine purr as it drove away.

Jackson hung the halter on the rack and flipped the light switch. Darkness enveloped him until his eyes grew accustomed to the night. As he walked toward the house, he thought about her safe in his bed, not with Paul.

He opened the screen door and walked into the muted light of the living room. She was sitting at the kitchen bar and when he entered, she stood.

"I need to talk to you," she said, her voice soft, so unlike her.

"Tomorrow."

"Not tomorrow. There are things I need to straighten out now, before I lose my nerve."

Jackson drew in a deep breath and went to the kitchen. He jerked the refrigerator door open and took the tea pitcher from it. Alexandria's full glass was on the bar before her. He glanced at it, got a glass for himself, and poured.

"Go ahead. But I'm tired, and remember we both have to get up early."

She sat back down at the bar, hoping he'd sit too, but he continued to stand over her. "I know you don't like me much right now, but I need to be direct with you." She stood and turned away, unable to watch him as she told him about Paul. "For as long as I can remember, I've always regarded power as security. Everything I've ever done was to make more money, to get more power, to be more secure. Paul is the same way, and for years we've worked together and understood each other perfectly. We have built a corporate business that has hardly a rival in the free world, and I've sunk everything I am into being APM Corporation. It always seemed a natural extension of our business relationship to marry, but, Jackson, I don't—"

"Look," his gravelly whisper interrupted. "You don't have to explain your engagement. You were perfectly clear about what you wanted from me."

She faced him. "You don't understand. Alexandria's found that Alex doesn't need APM or anything else to feel secure."

"Hey, careful, don't go out on a limb. Tomorrow you might regret it and want to change every word."

Guilt struck her like a sword through the heart. All the times she'd been drawn to him only to rebuff him the next moment had been so unfair. He stepped forward and she knew he wanted to touch her, but wouldn't.

"I know Paul's the reason you kept your distance, but tell me one thing, Alex." His voice hardened into a growl. "If you're in love with him, then why was that one kiss so good?"

She didn't know what to tell him.

"From the dead silence, I'd guess it was because it was all an act."

"No, you're wrong."

"I fell for it too."

"No," she protested weakly, shaking her head. "It was real."

"Save it," he held his hand up. "I'll know next time."

"Jackson, please," she touched his elbow.

He set her hand aside quickly but quietly. "Alexandria. Don't worry. I understand. We'll finish out the month and then we'll follow separate trails. I'm not mad, I just feel more foolish than I want to. You were right. You're not available. You're paying me for a service, and I was the one who overstepped the line."

"Jackson, please—"

"Relax. Now I understand."

CHAPTER 5

Alexandria wished *she* understood. OK. She hadn't told him she was engaged to Paul—she hadn't told him about Paul at all. But lying in bed every night, she hadn't seen that it was any of Jackson's business, especially since he seemed to pride himself on staying out of other people's affairs. *Why couldn't he practice what he preached*, she thought angrily as she rolled to her side.

Smashing her eyes closed, Alexandria still couldn't hide from the truth that she did feel guilty, like a puppy with a chewed slipper in its mouth, and she hated it. She wanted to go to sleep and start all over in the morning. *Fat chance*, she thought, rolling to the other side. She'd tried, without success, to sleep him into oblivion before, and the more she thought about the anger and the hurt in those damnable brown eyes of his, the more certain she was that the problem was going to be bigger and more real at dawn.

She heard him once during the night when he got up to get a drink from the kitchen and toyed with the idea of going out and trying to talk. When she heard him return to his office and to bed, a wave of revulsion for her own cowardice swept over her. She lay half sleeping, half awake the rest of the long night.

Finally, just before dawn, she heard him moving around. It was earlier than usual, but Jackson was up and fiddling in the kitchen. Alexandria dreaded facing him. As she dressed, she realized that somewhere, sometime in the short two weeks, it had become important that Jackson not think the worst of her. She stopped short with the doorknob in hand.

The one thing she knew for sure was that he was enough of a gentleman to ensure he would be polite, and having dealt in the business world, she supposed she could handle that. But what she feared more than she thought possible was losing the warmth she'd come to expect from her cowboy mentor. Since the first day he'd smiled, laughed, and had an easygoing kind of confidence. If he wasn't the same Jackson, if he was cold and distant—if he treated her the way she deserved—she wasn't sure she could stand it.

The knob grew hot in her hand. She forced a deep breath and prayed for courage. Stepping out, she looked toward the kitchen. His back was to her and she froze. He looked exactly like the Jackson she'd grown to—

To what? To depend on? To admire? To love?

No. She huffed a half-hearted laugh at herself. *Imagine the Queen of Corporate America being in love with a cowboy.* There was as little sense in that as there was in her being able to live in a mobile home for the rest of her life. It just wasn't realistic—or possible.

As if he sensed her presence, he slowly turned.

"You're up early. Ready for juice?" he said as if this were any other morning. "I've got an omelet in the making, but you can start on juice."

Alexandria stepped gingerly into the kitchen.

"Short practice today. I want to load things and make sure we've got everything for Rancho Murieta. You'll have to work Hattie, but I don't want you to cut, just leg her up and then maybe take her out. She'll be fresher for you if she hasn't worked a cow the day before." He waved a chef's knife as he talked. "She'll really want to work a cow after a day off."

"Jackson," she began, unable to deal with his cheery tone.

"Here." He tossed her a loaf of bread. "Toast a couple of slices."

She caught the plastic-wrapped loaf the same time she caught his gaze. For the longest time, neither said a word. He'd tossed a challenge her way—go back to the way it was, or fight. Alexandria wanted very much to go back to working together, to being warmed by his smile, and to enjoying his company.

She stuck two slices in the toaster. "Margarine in the refrigerator?" Alexandria Payne just backed down from a fight.

He reached for the tub of margarine near the cutting board and held it out to her.

She reached for it, but he held on to it.

"You look like hell."

"I beg your pardon?"

"You heard me. You look like hell." He released the tub and turned his attention to the heated skillet. "If you're going to do well tomorrow, you have to get more rest."

Normally it was she who pushed people beyond their limits to exhaustion. This was payback.

The toaster popped its product, and Alexandria buttered intently, her thoughts on anything but breakfast. She put two more slices in and sat down just as Jackson set a steaming omelet in front of her. He smiled.

"Eat. We'll get through the next two weeks if we both remember where we're going. Neither one of us can afford to dwell on mistakes. Shake it off."

Mistakes. His choice of words, but she knew better. "Jackson, I want to thank you…for making everything so easy, so comfortable."

He laughed as he reached for the coffeepot. "If I was good at making things comfortable, like you say, I'd damn sure make that sofa in the office a little more comfortable."

He poured her a cupful and caught her staring in bewilderment. "That was a joke."

As soon as Jackson drove into the Rancho Murieta equine complex, Alexandria was struck with stage fright. Small practice events had been exciting, but this was the real thing, and suddenly time was running out. If she didn't make it here, she wasn't going to be ready for Covington. There was a lot at stake.

She had a lot to lose with Jackson too. Not only was she haunted by his kiss and by the final way he'd told her to forget it, that he understood, but there was more. Casual talk with other cutters confirmed the fact that he trained; he didn't give lessons, private or otherwise, to anyone but her. The deal they'd finally negotiated for her use of his bedroom had, at the time, seemed a clear indication of his needing money, but turning down pupils didn't make sense. Everyone knew and liked him, and everyone was watching her to find out what was so special; it forced a strange sense of responsibility upon her.

Alexandria fumbled with the cinch before she mounted up, then struggled to focus in the warm-up pen. It wasn't at all like her, and frustration multiplied with each stride.

"Try giving her a little more rein," Jackson said, observing her stiffness. "Don't you see Hattie bobbing her head? She needs to be able to stretch out and loosen up."

Jackson knew all he had to do was ride close, touch Alex's shoulder, and she would relax. He also knew that was impossible. "Relax your hips and sit down. You're as tense as a porcupine in a balloon factory."

He saw her take a deep breath and settle into her seat, then toss a half-hearted smile his way. That small gesture warmed him, and suddenly he swore he felt her lips, cool, soft, and addictive. Deep in his belly, a hunger gnawed at his gut. His neck and shoulders were stiff and sore from sleeping on the couch in the office, and his mind was stiff and sore from yearning for the hot, sensual woman he'd kissed. Two weeks was a long time to go without touching her. Two weeks until she was gone.

He tipped his head and forced a smile for her.

"Jackson, darling." Trisha galloped a flashy paint to his side and slid to a stop, completing a showy entrance. She leaned over and kissed his cheek. "You bad boy, I was expecting you at my party Saturday."

He legged his horse away from her and walked out. "We were too tired to go out again."

Trisha's sweet expression was lost for an instant, replaced by a jealous pout, her luscious lips as impressive as ever. "You've just been spending all your free time with *her.* I don't mind admitting I'm a little bit envious and"—she trotted up and rode beside him—"I want to know what kind of hold she's got on you, Jackson Morgan."

He smiled. If he could tell her what hold Alex had on him, then they would both know. It wasn't as simple as that, and had he known when Hesperia called that he'd be in this predicament, he doubted he would have accepted—money or not. He looked to Trisha, who waited expectantly for his reply.

"She's got nothing on me, Trisha. It was a case of being in the right place at the right time."

"Jackson," she tugged at his arm, halting them both. "Do you need money?"

"No," he said quickly and rode on.

She caught up. "I'm serious. I have plenty of money, and I'm really sorry about the fine and the lawsuit. Do you need money for—"

"I told you, no. I paid it all and everything's right."

"Well, if you're sure."

"I'm sure. The only thing I have to worry about is whether or not you can beat my horse in the novice class."

Trisha laughed. "Oh, Jackson, you'd better get a deep seat, because this little horse can spin on a dime."

"Well, mine is faster than greased lighting, and I'd be willing to wager we'll beat you by a point and a half or better," he answered, grateful she'd followed him to another subject.

"You're on," she said as she picked up her reins and spurred the paint into a lope. "I'll be around to collect my winnings."

Jackson saw Trisha skid to a stop next to Ray Mueller, a trainer from down south. Although she didn't greet him with a kiss, he knew Ray was hearing the same flirtatious lines and suffering the same bold attack. The difference was he knew Ray was probably lapping it up. For a moment he wished he could shine it on too. He wished he was the kind of person who could ride from face to face and deliver flirtatious lines the whole way. But he'd never been that kind of person and he'd never put much stock in bragging. If he was on top, and he was, it was due to hard work and skill; he wouldn't trade that for all the fluff in the world.

Urging the palomino mare into a lope, Jackson kept an eye out for Alex. She must have forgotten something at the trailer, since she was nowhere to be seen. By the time she returned, he was warmed up and waiting for his turn in the novice class. She was still nervous. He wanted to go talk her into confidence and relaxation, but that would have to wait since Trisha was up and he was riding turn back.

Trisha rode well, but she never would have the kind of competence it took to let the horse free up and work the cow. She scored a seventy-two, but the paint should have scored higher. Jackson came out of the pen, positive his palomino could do better. Minutes later, as he entered for his turn, the familiar thrill shot through him just like it did every time he began to compete. The palomino was born and bred to cut and she knew it was her turn to shine. Ears pointed, every step showed her desire to work a cow. The first time he entered the herd, she was a little too eager, but he settled deep in the saddle and calmed her with one hand on her neck.

Three cows stayed to the outside when Jackson picked the one he wanted, and the mare made the sort as smoothly and calmly as a seasoned competitor. The red cow eyed the horse and rider and moved hesitantly to the right, then darted to the left. The palomino waited for a commitment and then reacted flawlessly to it, following perfectly, sticking to its hip.

The cow started getting a little wild-eyed and Jackson pulled up easily; he went to the herd in search of a better one.

Alexandria sat ringside, mesmerized by Jackson's competence on the green palomino. She'd seen him work the horse from day one and was impressed. The second cow he picked to work was a black white face that tried to squeeze past the corner turn back. As she guessed he would do, Jackson made a few good cuts and then let the cow return to the herd.

Midway through his third cow, the whistle blew and Jackson pulled up, dropping the reins as he exited amid the applause of the crowd. The announcer reported Jackson's score, a seventy-six. He dismounted and loosened the cinch while a tall, lean man approached him from behind. His back was to Alexandria, but she was pretty sure she hadn't seen him before.

The man wore a crisp white shirt and a silver-belly hat. He tapped Jackson on the shoulder. When Jackson turned, a wide, eager smile broke out all over his face, and he grasped the older man's arm, pulling him into an enthusiastic hug.

"Alex," Jackson called out. "Come here. I've got someone I want you to meet."

Before Jackson had finished the invitation, the older man turned. Alexandria's pulse quickened when she saw James Covington, as big as all of Texas and smiling twice as boldly. Moving between several horses, Alexandria closed in on her target. She almost felt faint. Things were falling into place perfectly.

"Alex. This is the man who taught me most of what I know. This is Everett Covington. Ev, meet Alexandria Payne."

Covington extended his hand to her, and when they shook it was like the mountain meeting Mohammed. Before her stood the man who previously had been unavailable to APM Corporation. The business world knew him as James, but it appeared his cronies knew him as Everett. This was Jackson's mentor. If only she'd put two and two together sooner, she would have been a good deal more interested in what went on between Everett and Jackson. She was going to enjoy telling Paul facts that his "extensive" research missed.

"Pleasure to meet you, young lady. I hear you're puttin' Jackson here through his paces."

"Nice to meet you too, Everett," she said, sharpening her claws. "I'm guessing from your delightful drawl that you're from Texas?"

"Can't hide nothin' from a smart woman," he grinned. "You'd better keep your eye on this one, sonny."

Alexandria wanted to continue the conversation, but her class was called and Jackson reminded her to go get ready.

"I'm gonna buy you two dinner after this pea shoot is over, so go give it your best and we'll watch."

Another stroke of luck. A friendly dinner was perfect to get to know the old codger, whom she judged to be considerably less formidable than Paul had led her to believe. He had a friendly face and a seemingly jovial nature, but the war wasn't won yet. She still had a lot of work to do, the least of which was her turn in the cutting pen.

By the time her name was called, Alexandria was refreshed and focused. She rode through the gate like a crusader riding into battle. Out of the corner of her eye, she saw Jackson and Everett. How ironic that the two men with whom she had been consumed sat side by side in the bleachers, both waiting for her to ride, both wishing her success, and both unaware of how each played into her plan.

Jackson smiled and nodded, offering a special kind of moral support only he could give. Alexandria rode into the pen with renewed confidence. She felt strong and bold. Thousands of things that Jackson had told her in the course of lessons ran through her mind one by one at warp speed. Almost on automatic, Hattie slowly made her way into the herd and began the sort. Alexandria tried to remember everything about a cow, the way it held its head, the way it moved among the others, the way the eye looked as it was cut off from the rest. Finally she had one separated from the herd and Hattie settled into her job.

If it hadn't been for the experience of the mare, Alexandria might still be standing, looking at the herd. The mare made her look good and she knew it. A thousand pounds of horse moved like a five-pound cat under her, and it was exhilarating. Each and every move felt as if her soul took flight.

Suddenly Alex wondered how long she'd spent on that one cow. She waited carefully until the right moment and then pulled Hattie off. She'd been lost in the thrill, but now she realized she had to wake up and help the horse.

Her second sort was for a brindle-colored cow that hid its head among the others. Hattie made the separation without flaw, and then as she began to work, Alexandria fell out of time. *Just stay in the middle of the horse*, she reminded herself, but no matter what she did, it never felt as good as the first work; she couldn't get with the flow.

After a few seconds working the brindle cow, she realized it was pretty high-headed and wild. Hattie was doing a good job of keeping up, but the cow was quick and hard to predict. About thirty seconds had passed when the horn blew and time was up.

She raised her hand, reined Hattie in, and rode out past Trisha, who flashed an insincere smile and congratulations. Alexandria was shaking as she rode toward the trailer, but she couldn't hide the smile that broke out all over her face. She hadn't fallen off. She hadn't lost the cow. Life was great. She felt like shouting; she felt like dancing. It was better than closing a big deal.

At the trailer, she dismounted and hugged Hattie's neck. Hattie nuzzled her back, and as Alexandria stroked her soft cheek, it hit her how attached to the mare and to this cutter's life she'd grown.

Jackson walked up and saw Alex, not Alexandria. Ever since Paul's visit, he'd told himself that Alexandria was sleeping in his bed, sharing his meals, unavailable, unapproachable, and untouchable. He'd resigned himself to deal with Alexandria, but right now, seeing Alex cuddled up to Hattie, smiling and fresh from a good ride, he wasn't sure he could separate the two.

"Congratulations."

She spun around, still smiling. "I was more nervous than I thought, Jackson, but I made it." She ran her fingers through Hattie's glossy mane. "Of course, it was all Hattie. I—"

"Did you stay long enough to hear your score?"

She looked up, stricken. "No. I forgot. Did you hear it?"

"I certainly did." He stuffed his hands in his pockets and rocked back and forth on his toes and heels like a little boy.

"Well?" she asked, now impatient. "What did we score?"

"Seventy-four. You probably have the class won."

"Oh, Jackson!" She leaped into his arms and wrapped herself around him. "Thank you. I can't believe it. Things just kept running through my mind and I wasn't sure of anything except that Hattie would take care of me."

Her body fit his perfectly, and when his arms wrapped around her, he closed his eyes and imagined her as his. He'd been prepared to teach, to tell her that she'd spent way too much time with the first cow and to warn her about picking the pistol out of the herd, but now that seemed the farthest thing from his mind.

"I knew you'd do well, Alex," he said softly as he memorized the feel and smell of her.

"A seventy-four! I can't believe it!" she squealed as she pushed away. "That's pretty good, isn't it?"

A nod and a smile were his only answer. Her success at her first show was something to celebrate, but it also was another step toward her leaving.

"That land lizard!"

Jackson and Alex turned to find Everett walking their way. "Lizard?" Alexandria asked, suddenly cautious and looking around.

"A Brahma crossbred, like that brindle second cow. But never mind all that. Good job, young lady. Put up your horse and let's get to dinner. I'm so hungry I could eat a folded tarp."

Throughout dinner and over the next two days, Alexandria had the feeling that Everett was watching her like a hawk. Brushing a horse or warming up, or once even when she was reading—times when she thought she was alone—she'd turn or look up and find him watching from afar. Sometimes he'd acknowledge her when their eyes met; sometimes he'd pretend he hadn't seen her.

Alexandria had the urge to question him, but what would she say? *Are you watching me? Why are you looking at me?* Everything sounded pretty self-centered and any answer he might give was bound to be innocent and harmless.

Each time she spoke to Paul, she mentioned Covington's interest, and he assured her that it was only a man's interest in a beautiful woman that made Covington watch her. Alexandria was not convinced, but had nothing solid to go on.

"I'm sure there is some real connection between Covington and Jackson, I'm just not able to put my finger on it. They talk like they've known each other for years."

"My check on Jackson gives his father's and mother's names, and neither of them had living relatives. My guess is that they are just cutting horse chums and that you worry too much."

Alexandria heard his impatience over the phone and bristled. "I worry because you guess too much and guessing isn't good enough to make COMJET a reality. I don't want to be caught unaware as we both were in the beginning."

"You're getting more snippy every time I speak with you, Alexandria. I do believe country life doesn't agree with you."

But country life *did* agree with her. There were parts of her that had never been happier, working with real things, dealing with concrete problems like which way the cow was going and... she stopped herself before finishing. And being with Jackson.

"Alexandria. Yoohoo, Alexandria!"

"What?"

"I said it's a pure stroke of luck that Covington is right there in your ever-so-capable hands. Have you been able to draw him into your confidence?"

"Weren't you listening, Paul? I don't think Covington is a man who can be led by the nose. I don't want to tip our hand too soon..."

The day before Everett left, he found her sitting on a stool in the tack room cleaning Hattie's bridle. At first she thought he would pass her by as usual, but surprisingly, he stopped to talk.

"Gotcha hard at work, huh, little lady?" He leaned against the doorjamb, running his fingers into the tight Wrangler pockets that hugged his slender hips. The morning sun behind him sent hot rays into the tack room and silhouetted him like the financial god he was. "Clean tack says something about a person."

She tilted her head and smiled as she looked toward him. "And what does it say about me?"

He crossed his arms and raised one brow. "Maybe a lot, maybe a little."

Chuckling to herself at the vague response, she replied, "You mean a lot if you can read my mind, a little if you can't."

"You're a sharp lady. I would like to know what's inside your head, but I'm afraid I might not like what I hear."

She stopped.

She laid the heavy leather reins in her lap and looked directly at Everett. "Why don't you ask and maybe you'll like what I have to say."

Eyes narrowed, he stood tall, not moving a muscle; she could see him thinking, plotting his strategy, and instantly knew she might have made the fatal mistake of underestimating the quiet Texan. He reminded her of Wyatt Earp at the OK Corral, cunning, ready for battle.

Finally he uncrossed his arms and moved deliberately into the tack room, fingering several expensive silver bits as he strolled to the other side of the cramped room. He turned to face her. "You know, Jackson was only a boy when I first met him."

Finally she was going to find out what that special connection was between Jackson and Everett. Like a skilled bargainer, Alex sat quietly and let him talk.

"He was in a juvenile detention home and felt like the whole world had spit on him. I needed ranch help and he was one of the oldest, and the only one who looked like he might handle a manure fork, so he came to live with me."

Alexandria leaned back, intrigued. "So you taught him how to ride a horse?"

Everett smiled, then continued. "Nope. He already knew how to ride. All I had to do was steer him in the right direction." He stared into the past as he spoke and his face softened in love. "He was a pistol, all right. He was hungry to be the best and there wasn't a blade of grass gonna grow under his feet."

He looked to her, and to disguise her interest, she immediately picked up the rein and rubbed saddle soap into the fine leather. "He's still the same. If there's a minute of spare time, he has a book to read, a video to watch, or," she held up the reins, "odd jobs to do."

Everett said nothing until she finally looked back to him. "I've never seen him smile so much."

Alexandria was caught in Everett's tough-as-nails gaze. "I wouldn't know," she said, suddenly wary.

"He's always been solid as a rock." He shifted position, his hand dropping to a saddle on the rack and his back to her. "If he ever falls for some gal, he's gonna fall hard."

Alexandria felt as if she'd been hit by an avalanche. She was sure Everett said something else before he left, but couldn't remember what. The only thing she remembered was the way her heart beat in her throat and the way "he's gonna fall hard" was burned into her soul.

The rules of the game had changed. Things had become complicated, and she was having trouble sorting fact from fiction. Illogically, the only thing she was sure of was the way she felt when Jackson kissed her. Fire raged inside her, and nothing she said or did seemed able to douse the intense sense of excitement when she recalled how it felt to be branded by his touch.

Suddenly she was on shaky ground. The footing was bad and the cow was wild. Her mind was out of control and Jackson Morgan was the reason.

Everett Covington left for Texas as suddenly as he'd come. Alexandria angrily relayed what she'd found out about Jackson and Covington to Paul, who was overjoyed with the prospect of a deeper, more reliable connection for Alexandria to follow. She argued that Paul's failure to expose the real connection between the two cowboys increased the danger of the deal blowing up in their faces. After she hung up, she quizzed herself. Was it the deal that worried her most or the fact that Jackson would consider any move on the man he called father a betrayal?

Paul called her Sunday morning at Rancho Murieta and again at noon, when Jackson's final cut was about to begin. Each time he became more insistent that she take quick advantage of her strategically perfect position. Each time he insisted she became less willing and more resentful of his persistence.

"I'll do this in my own time," she said impatiently.

"Alexandria. You're getting soft. I can't believe you, the Wall Street barracuda, is sitting on this opportunity."

"And you aren't here. You don't know what's happening. This is not Wall Street where people can be bullied. You tried and got nowhere with Covington. Now leave me to handle this." Alexandria hung up feeling like a trained bear, under pressure to perform.

Jackson's performance was flawless, however; the entire weekend, he'd been supportive, friendly, and wonderful. But he'd kept everything on a purely business-as-usual basis, and Alexandria had finally accepted that she wanted more. She wanted more long, passionate kisses that built toward an explosion of the senses, and she wanted romance. She wanted the fairy tale. She wanted to see how Jackson would wake her in the morning. Would he kiss her awake or would he touch and tease her awake?

Yes, the rules had changed.

CHAPTER 6

The day after their triumphant return from Rancho Murieta Paul came to the ranch. He arrived just before lunch as Alexandria and Jackson were putting up horses for the morning.

The indoor arena and barn were beginning to heat up and Alexandria had worked hard enough to be looking forward to relaxing at lunch with Jackson. She had pulled the saddle from her horse and put it away in the tack room while Jackson went to the wash rack to rinse the sweat from his horses. She had heard Jackson speaking to someone other than Juan, but when Paul appeared, dressed impeccably as usual, she was caught off guard.

"Hello, darling." He stared intently at her as he stepped forward and politely kissed her cheek. "I checked with Jackson and he says you're free for the rest of the day. I thought we'd go to the Slocum House for a leisurely lunch."

"Um, I thought, well…" Her brows knit in question. "Are you sure Jackson said he had nothing for me to do later?" After being away there were lots of things they needed to catch up on, and she would much rather eat in the neat mobile home at the top of the hill with Jackson than finish her chores. That wouldn't work now that Paul had shown up.

"He said something about a horse, but I told him how lonely I've been without you; he agreed that we needed time together."

"Oh." She nodded slowly, reading between the lines and not liking it.

Suddenly Jackson appeared, as if he'd been waiting around the corner until Paul had outlined his plans. He had two glistening, wet horses in hand and spoke as he led them toward the hot walker. "You know, Alex—"

The use of her nickname was a firm reminder of where she was and where she wanted to be.

"I forgot all about having to go to Sacramento early tomorrow, and I'm sure it'll take a while, so why don't you just take a day off? We'll get started again Wednesday."

"But, I thought—"

Paul wrapped a supportive arm around her. "Now, darling, you have been working much too hard. You're brown as a coffee bean, which tells me how much time you've spent in the damaging sun." He looked from her to Jackson. "And Jackson agrees you need a break."

Alexandria met Jackson's steely gaze and winced when she heard him say, "Go ahead. I understand." His voice was slow and seductive. "If I was in love with a woman, I wouldn't want to be apart as long as you have. See you Wednesday."

I understand. Again. She watched him walk back out into the sun toward the hot walker. The afternoon promised one hundred-degree weather, but the chill was obvious.

"Good." Paul smoothed the front of his suit as he faced her. "I'm going to whisk you away from this hot, desolate dust bowl and treat you to not only lunch, but to a very expensive dinner, and I'm going to lavish excessive gifts and treats upon you."

Alexandria just stood and looked at Paul. When had she lost control of the situation and at what point had she become unsure of what she really wanted? Alexandria reached for the lead rope. "But first, I have to finish with my horse." One after another she conjured up tasks necessary to finish before she left. Finally, taking a deep breath, she turned and looked at Paul, standing ramrod stiff, impatient as he waited for her.

Things had changed. It was obvious that she and Paul needed to talk. Perhaps this afternoon was the perfect opportunity. It was simple. *Seize the moment.* Put Paul in his place and let him know that he'd already taken too many liberties and assumed too much in a relationship that she had controlled very nicely prior to James Everett Covington and Jackson.

"I'll wash up and change at the house," she said as she started up the driveway. "I'll only be a minute. You can come if you like."

"I have a few calls to make; I'll wait for you in the car."

Alexandria hurried once she found Jackson was very conveniently nowhere to be seen, and within ten minutes she emerged in shorts and got in the black BMW.

The air conditioner was running; the cool air hit her and sent a shiver through her body as she settled in and fastened her seat belt. Paul was on his cell phone and shifted into reverse as he spoke. "We're on our way now. Have everything ready when we arrive."

The wheels of the car crunched on the gravel as Paul gassed it, and soon the barns were out of sight. Alexandria sat quietly, willing herself to focus on what she was going to say to Paul rather than on the fact that she was leaving what felt like home.

"I have a ream of papers for you to sign and there are some decisions I've made that I want to check out with you," Paul said as he urged the car on through the gentle curves of the golden, rolling hills. "There is a small glitch in that deal with Creative Labs, but I have talked to people who owe us favors and I think it will be no problem. Did you know that the CEO at Branson Limited committed suicide?" He hardly waited for an answer before he went on. "Poor schmuck got caught with his hand in the till and couldn't handle it. Branson will be vulnerable, and I thought we should look into it. Are you listening, Alexandria? I said Branson looks good."

She hadn't really been listening at all, but she turned and stared at him. "I heard every word. Branson looks good and you have Creative Labs under control." She twisted in her seat to face him. "Paul. I need to talk to you about—"

"Oh yes," he interrupted, "another tidbit you'll be glad to hear. Hesperia told me the other day that she heard stock is about to fall—"

"Paul. I said I wanted to talk. Now be quiet and listen. I don't know exactly what you said to Jackson, but I want you to back off. I—"

"You what, Alexandria?" he said more testily than usual. "You're getting in over your head."

"No," she sighed. "I'm not. The only problem I'm experiencing is your arrogant presumption that you can snap your fingers and I'll be there."

"Arrogant? Me?" He stiffened in his seat and pushed the pedal to the floor. "We are engaged, Alexandria. You have been living with this man for almost three weeks now and I'm not supposed to be resentful?"

"I don't want to argue with you over semantics."

"Semantics! Just which word isn't clear?" He raced down the road into the bedroom community of Rancho Murieta where he slowed and turned off the main road, heading for the airport. He ground the gears as he slowed near the runway where the smallest APM jet waited.

Alexandria closed her eyes and held her breath for a moment, trying to collect her thoughts, planning the appropriate coolness in her voice. "I am not living with anyone in the sense you imply, and you know that. As far as being engaged goes…" She tilted her head back as he stopped, then slowly lowered her face as if she were taking aim at him. "That is a condition that needs to be resolved."

The color drained ever so slightly from his face as he turned off the motor. "All right. I agree we need to talk. But let's do it in the comfort of the plane. I called ahead and made reservations at that wonderful little bed and breakfast in Carmel that you adore so, and a gourmet lunch is waiting on the plane."

Alexandria crossed her arms over her chest and remained silent.

"Please. You know how I detest fighting with you. After nearly eleven years of working together, we've ironed out every problem we've ever had. Come," he held out his hand to her, "relax with me for a day." He glanced at her from head to toe. "You really need a trip to the spa. Your arms and legs look like they belong to different people, and the sun is so bad for your skin."

She drew a deep breath and sighed again. She was losing it, all right. The cutting edge, the instinctive will to tear an opponent apart was becoming veiled by a ridiculous sense of fairness. It should have been disgusting to her, but at the moment, the only disgusting part of her situation was that she took his hand and nodded. Working with him would be murder if she didn't find a way to let him down easily.

The next thing she knew, deliciously soft Italian leather seats enveloped her and the ring of fine crystal floated as Paul toasted their success. The wine was positively wonderful. The feeling of power was once again overwhelming. Paul was like a child in his delight.

"Try this pâté. It's positively wonderful."

The engines roared as they left the runway headed for Monterey, the closest airport to the quaint little areas surrounding Pacific Grove and Carmel, the places she used to love above all else.

"Paul." She set the crystal wine glass down. "About this engagement thing. Originally, we..."

He covered her hand on the armrest, sat back, and looked at her in earnest. He lifted his glass high again. "To you, Alexandria. You're more woman than I ever realized." He drank heavily, then returned the glass to his lap, running a finger around the lip.

"Originally, we got engaged pretty much for business purposes, but I know things have changed."

Alexandria dropped her gaze to her own lap. "Yes. Something has changed, Paul. I don't know when, but it has."

Suddenly he was on his knees before her, grinning, gushing. "Then marry me, Alexandria. Marry me right now. This engagement has gone on long enough."

She stared into his handsome, eager face and pushed him away. His proposal was both comic and tragic. "No, no. This is not where I thought this conversation was going." She shook her head. "I don't want to be engaged any longer, Paul. I—"

"But we work so well together." His expression was incredulous. "We're a team. We understand each other."

She leaned forward and looked directly into his eyes. "We will still be a team, Paul; nothing will change except that you and I will be free, personally."

The pained look on his face as he sat back in the chair appeared to be very real, but she wondered. He was as tough as she ever was, and she knew that, given the right circumstances, she too could have presented a suitably wounded look. However, he had been there for her for over ten years, and he had been an undeniable force in her life. She also knew for certain that she didn't love him.

"I must not be understanding you."

"I think you understand, but you're not comprehending, Paul. The engagement is over." Even as she told him they would still be a team, the thought echoed in her mind that that couldn't be the same either.

He ran his hand over his forehead and down the side of his face, curtaining her view of his features. Like a mime, his expression changed. "Of course." The arrogance had returned. "I understand completely. And you're right. I apologize." He seemed to breathe more slowly and more calmly. "I'll call ahead and reserve a second room while you look over those papers I mentioned earlier. Be sure to check the Creative Lab ones carefully." He stood and took several file folders from a briefcase. As he handed them to her, she swore he was going to say something, but he remained silent. He walked to the far end of the cabin, and as Alexandria perused the tedious business agreements, she heard his muted voice on the phone.

After several minutes he returned and began as if nothing had ever been spoken about their personal relationship. "I hope you're making progress with Covington. We've sunk a substantial amount of time and money into COMJET, and we are at the point of no return, so to speak. We need him."

She continued to read. "I told you, we have fallen into a remarkably good place. He is a mentor to Jackson, and we never could have gotten this close even if we had planned it out."

"We're running out of time."

She looked up. "The climax and test of my month of training is going to be some show down south—Temecula, I believe. I'm going to prove my worth; Jackson is showing, as is Covington. I'll close the deal there."

The silence between them was ominous. Neither read the other as well as before and neither trusted the other. Things had changed.

Alexandria threw open the double doors that led to a small private balcony. The ocean air rippled her long, flowing silk peignoir around her legs; it was refreshing after the heat and dryness of the interior valley. Paul had insisted she shop for everything she'd need for her escape, and although the silk felt heavenly, shopping in the cute little boutiques wasn't as much fun as it could have been.

Alexandria had loved Carmel, even as a child. It was small, relaxed, and intimate compared to the highly impersonal setting of Los Angeles. Her father had always brought her here for her birthday. It was the one time a year he had made an effort to give face-to-face time to her. Little as it was, it was enough. Her father had been her hero, and his death had left a hole in her life that she filled by following in his footsteps. Her business career had been going well before, but after he was gone, Alexandria threw herself body and soul into the same things he loved.

Paul had been hired by her father, and it was no secret that no matter how well she did, her father had preferred a male heir. The logical corporate union between her and Paul was the last big celebration her father had been part of.

Carmel brought back years of memories, but those memories were not as comfortable as the little mobile home on the knoll.

Watching the waves pound the rocks, she pondered her next steps. Until Jackson Morgan, her life had been perfectly ordered and under control, with no doubts that she was doing what she wanted. Suddenly her once-solid goals were like a gossamer jellyfish caught in the surf, floating at the will of the tide, right side up, upside down, spinning, lost.

Somewhere a sea gull squawked. The sound of crashing surf surrounded her. She swore it whispered Jackson's name, but knew it was her own soul that had been etched with the way he laughed, the gentle way he touched, and the electric feel of his lips on hers.

How could two people meet and merge lives that had nothing in common?

She walked back into her room and sat amid the Laura Ashley flowers and Queen Anne elegance. This bed and breakfast was her favorite, and she had always come pretending she never had to leave. It had been her connection to what family she used to have, and her sanctuary from the bustle of the business rat race. Before, she had looked forward to expensive antiques, private dining, expert service, and peace and quiet. Today, however, even though the magnificent setting sun spread its rays across the beaches and boats dotting the lazy horizon, there was no peace and no quiet.

Noise from traffic nearby, unseen people talking, the clatter of dishes from somewhere below—sounds she never heard before were all around her, and somehow she knew there would be no peace until Jackson was with her. Again, the dilemma. As good as she had always been at getting things her way, how was she going to win the heart of a cowboy who had no interest in her way of life, who thought her kiss was a lie? What was going to happen when Jackson found out the real reason she had to learn to cut?

She knew she'd hurt Paul, that in his own possessive way, he did really care for her, but she also knew that no matter what happened with Jackson, she couldn't go back. Finishing what she started was a personal passion with her, but at the conclusion of the COMJET deal, she would have to decide what was going to happen to APM. She wouldn't bail out on Paul in the middle of a project, but it remained to be seen if APM would survive when the loose ends were all tied up.

If she couldn't win Jackson in her life, then where would she go if there was no APM? She didn't know how to do or be much else, except, of course, now she could ride a cutting horse. She pumped a short laugh at herself. Who was she kidding? If life ahead didn't include a certain trainer, then she didn't really want to cut. Everything had seemed so simple: buy a corporation, convert and rearrange it, sell the new product.

Simple.

Win a man's heart.

Not so simple.

She stood and looked away from the balcony. Perhaps a good, long soak in a bubble bath would clear her mind. She started for the bathroom when a knock came at the door.

She checked her watch and reassured herself it was too early for Paul to arrive for dinner. When she opened the door it was filled with red roses.

"Miss Payne." A small voice came from behind the blossoms. "Where would you like me to put these?"

"The dresser will be fine," Alexandria said, backing away from the moving mass of red.

Alexandria recognized the sweet chambermaid assigned to her room when she stepped out from behind the roses. "Thank you, Mary. They're beautiful. Can I assume they're from Mr. Maitland?"

"Yes, madam. He had them delivered after hours especially for you." She bowed as she pulled the door closed and left.

"Never send one when you can afford a dozen," she said, smiling as she walked over and smelled the bouquet. There was a profusion of bloom and aroma as she searched for the card.

"A dozen roses for each week you were gone.
Partners never come as good as you."
As ever, Paul

He really knew how to lay on the guilt, she thought as she tossed the card on the dresser, except that he forgot to sign it with love. Not that she wasn't the pot calling the kettle black; she was just as adept at manipulation, but lately the pride in using it was not what it had been.

He had forgotten to add love. *Call a spade a spade*, she thought to herself, agreeing to postpone the rest of her soul-searching until after dinner. Paul would be here soon, and she needed to shower and dress. When they had arrived earlier that afternoon, Paul had accompanied her shopping for suitable evening clothes. He was remarkably flexible that way. She couldn't imagine Jackson agreeing to shop for women's clothes, much less enjoying it.

Forty-five minutes later, she and Paul went to dinner at a restaurant that would have frowned on shorts, pants, or even a sundress. Alexandria was as far away from sweaty saddle pads, snotty-nosed cows, and Jackson Morgan as it was physically possible to get.

The sun was setting the next day when Paul dropped Alexandria off at the mobile home on the hill. He didn't try to kiss her goodbye, he didn't hold her hand a bit too long, and he didn't pretend she was still his. He was sweet and gentlemanly, and Alexandria was struck by a wave of guilt followed by a stab of suspicion.

Watching Paul drive away brought no feeling other than relief, but she turned to the door and realized she had to face Jackson. Assuming he was inside since she hadn't seen him by the barns on her way in, she opened the screen door and entered.

She called his name but got no answer.

The small house was still and that odd mixture of warm and cool air that happens when windows are opened in the evening after a hot day kissed her arms and bare shoulders as she walked to the kitchen bar. He'd left a note. "Riding. Back Soon. Jackson."

His handwriting was bold, yet boyish. Alexandria ripped the note from the pad and pressed it to her chest. Was it her imagination that she felt his wit and the warmth of his touch in this slip of paper, or was it wishful thinking? She had come looking for the magic key to Covington and had instead found the man who held the key to her heart. She felt as if she had crossed a bridge and that bridge had washed out behind her, the erosion so slow at first that she hadn't even noticed, but when it collapsed, there was no mistaking it.

Time was running out. In three days they were set to leave for Temecula and in three days she had to figure out how to juggle business, horses, and love. She took the pen next to the notepad by the phone and wrote the only thing she could think of at the moment. "I'm back. See you in the morning." The lovesick child in her wanted to sign it with her love or with Xs and Os, but the woman, wary of rejection, knew better.

"Are you going to sleep all day?"

Alexandria blinked and tried to sit up. The rising sun flashed brilliantly through the window, nearly blinding her. Jackson stood illuminated by the light in her half-opened door, glaring.

"I must have forgotten to set the alarm," she said, her voice crackling, still blinking as she rolled out of bed. Leaving the tender, whispering Jackson in her dreams, all she heard in her haste to get up was the gruff taskmaster Jackson. If she had been wider awake, she might have noticed the way his hungry eyes devoured her, then gave up quickly before he was found out.

"Enough vacation. We've got a lot to do if we're going to be ready for Temecula. I brought a new horse in yesterday, and I have to ride her this morning before I ride the others." He started to pull the door closed but stopped. He would have liked to say something nice, but he quickly reminded himself theirs was a business deal, nothing more.

"Toast and cold cereal are about all you have time for. I'll see you at the barn." He closed her door behind him and leaned against it. Alex tied his tongue and jumbled his mind and frustrated his soul and heated his body. He pushed off and headed for the barn, determined to find balance between her and what was left of his sanity.

Alexandria hurried, knowing Jackson would be waiting for her. He never asked about Paul, but she was sure Jackson assumed the worst. She jogged toward the barn, more intent upon catching up on lost time than worrying, only to find he was already saddled and warming up.

"Sorry I'm late," she called out as she went to get the lazy roan mare.

"Not my problem if you want to waste the best hours to ride sleeping." He dropped the gelding he rode into a smooth, flat lope and was quickly out of hearing distance.

Alexandria knew she'd been chastised again and also knew from the tone of his voice that she could look forward to a rigorous practice session. Hurrying to saddle up, she set the tone of her workout. Instead of allowing the mare to walk to the arena, she spurred her into a short, rough trot and hurried through the gate. As she latched it, she looked over to Jackson, whose sour expression was not comforting.

"Take your time. You're pushing that mare like she was the one who was late."

"You're right, sorry." Alexandria mounted and walked down the rail to the left, away from Jackson. She thought she had taken her time when she began to trot, but his coarse voice cut the silence.

"I want to see that horse relax more at the walk. If you push it now, you'll buzz her up and have to ride a long time to calm her. The harder you use your reins, the higher her head gets, and then she can't smooth out and be supple."

Alexandria had heard that speech over and over in the beginning, but not much lately. She sat back, dropped her reins, and rubbed her neck.

"Headache?" he asked as he rode by, more a statement than a question.

"Just a little."

He gave no reply but continued at a slow, very relaxed lope, offering himself as an example of the kind of pure, serene, easygoing movement she was looking for.

By lunch, he'd worked her mercilessly, putting her on five different horses when she usually rode three. There wasn't much satisfaction in his role as slave driver, but he was unable to stop. Admirably, she was up to the challenge, and although she was obviously hot, tired, and disgusted, she never whined or broke stride, which made him feel more like a dog than ever.

Over and over during lunch on the porch in the shade of the huge oak, Jackson tried to relax. He was irritable, and even the simplest of things came out much too edgy and brittle. He knew how he sounded, but it was impossible to do otherwise. The woman was driving him crazy, and he was powerless to defend himself.

The worst of it was that even when she should have taken him to task for his snippiness, she didn't. She acquiesced to his every wish, making him feel more the heel, more guilty with every word. Later, as he schooled Alexandria his efforts to be patient were fruitless. They had worked an hour or more, and all living things were hot and tired. He had just put her on a new horse, one that had a few lazy habits, and the herd was beginning to sour in the heat.

"No. You can't change your mind," he bit into her. "Once you pick a cow from the herd, you have to go with that one."

"I didn't change my mind," she said, finally showing a little spunk. "The second cow just leaped ahead and then what was I to do? Let it go?"

"You have to be able to read them better than that," he answered, happy that she had finally come back at him. "Next time take that brown cow a little way down the fence before you quit. You need to get that horse to work out a little farther from the herd. He wants to get in too close."

He watched Alexandria grit her teeth and move into the herd. The brown cow in question wanted to hide among the rest and she was having a terrible time making the cut. He should have seen and understood her problem.

"Get aggressive," he prodded instead. "Go in there and make it happen," Jackson added, his humorless growl digging at Alexandria the way her spurs dug at her mount to urge him on. "Go. Don't stop now."

"I'm doing the best I can," she answered impatiently.

"Don't quit on that horse now. He needs to get it together. You both are capable of doing it; you just have to cowboy up!"

Alexandria pulled the horse to a stop, threw the reins on his neck, and slapped one arm across the other.

"That's right, pout," he said, his voice softening despite the look on his face. "You aren't going to get good by giving up. I thought Alexandria Payne never gave up and never lost."

She looked his way and shot the most scathing silent reprimand she had left in her. Sweat was pouring off her face, and her clothes stuck to her body. He looked calm and cool. It wasn't fair. "I need a break. I'm exhausted."

"You had a whole day-and-a-half break. You should have been resting instead of—"

"Instead of what?" She spat the words at him. "That's what's really bothering you, isn't it? You're jealous that I went somewhere and maybe had a good time? What do *you* do to have a good time, huh, Jackson? Or maybe you never do?" The dam had broken and the words came tumbling out in a rush of breathless, pent-up emotion. "You drive yourself and everyone around you looking for that perfect cut. Is that why you have no other students? Because they can't cut it, literally or figuratively."

The silence was as heavy as the stale air in the indoor arena. For what seemed like minutes, but was seconds in reality, they stared at each other, the only sounds that of the breathing animals and the stomping of the stock. There was something in his eyes that told her she was on the verge of going too far.

She silently cursed herself. For a woman who wanted to impress a man, she was sure going about it the wrong way. "I'm sorry." She picked up her reins. "Move the brown cow down the fence," she said almost to herself as she moved away.

Jackson watched her work into the herd and try to separate the belligerent brown cow. He had told her to take that particular cow as a test and knew she would have a devil of a time moving it away from the herd. The horse she rode was not going to be a help either. He almost reneged and told her to take another cow, but his pride had been hurt and she had come dangerously close to prying into matters he considered private.

Scrutinizing her every move, Jackson wanted to lighten the mood. "Come on, you'll have to do better than that. I was going to challenge you to a match at Temecula, who scores highest, but I don't think you're up to it."

"You're on," she answered in haste, still watching the brown cow hunt for a way out. "The pupil will whip the professor."

The brown cow challenged her, and Jackson reveled in the fact that she met the challenge and was, in fact, beginning to move the brown cow away. Just a little farther down the rail and he would call her off.

Suddenly the brown monster turned and charged the horse, which panicked and tried to run backwards and sideways at the same time. Alexandria sat the storm well, but as the horse began crow hopping, she lost a stirrup. The cow, now on the prod and unwilling to quit, continued to attack.

Jackson spurred up and rode closer, but not so close that he added to the wreck. Alexandria's horse writhed in fear and anger, and as the brown cow smacked into its shoulder, things fell apart.

Alexandria's body swung wide to the left, in the direction she had no stirrup for support, and she fell off.

Jackson was already on the ground and running toward her.

The cow narrowly missed stepping on her. The horse shied and ran.

It all happened so fast there was hardly time to think, but the one thing that entered and stuck in Jackson's mind was that she might be hurt and that it was his fault.

He ran to her as she sprawled across the cool dirt, face first. Kneeling, he grabbed her shoulders and carefully turned her to him, cradling her in his arms. "My God, Alex, what have I done? Are you all right? Please, you've got be all right."

Spitting dirt, she groaned and began to move.

"No." He held her tight, afraid of what might have happened. "Be still a minute and just breathe. I'm so sorry."

Alexandria suddenly was quiet. Tears slid down her cheeks. She wanted so very much to be here in his strong arms, but she also wanted passion, not fright, to be the reason.

He released his hold on her as she sat up.

"You *are* hurt." A tortured look spread over his face. "We're done for today, Alex. I pushed you too hard and I'm sorry."

"No, I..." she whispered while she rotated first one shoulder then the other, "I'm OK. I'm fine," she said, sounding less than positive. "Just a little roughed up, perhaps, but I think I'm all right."

He wiped an errant wisp of hair from her face. His work-roughened fingers brushed dirt from her cheek, then loitered near like a starving man stays near a banquet table.

His eyes met hers and it was understood that the moment was theirs. No one was thinking about money, neither was thinking about anything except the other. His hand moved to her neck and pulled her closer.

"Shhh." He supported her chin with his thumbs and tipped her face toward his. "I knew that cow was trouble. I'm so sorry I did this to you," he whispered, his gruff tone music to her ears. "I want to kiss away the hurt."

She leaned into him, thankful he was close and thankful the wait was over. The first kiss was so gentle, she thought she was dreaming. His lips were warm as the summer breeze, and unlike the first kiss weeks ago, Alexandria wasn't thinking about how impossible he was. Her body was screaming for more and whatever sensibility she once possessed had evaporated like the morning mist.

One kiss led to another and another.

"Alex is back," he said, his mouth moving hungrily over her throat as she stretched like a cat enjoying the miracle of his touch.

"Yes," she agreed, both mentally and verbally. "Alex is back and loving everything about horses, cutting, this place, and..." Her fingers touched his cheek and then his lips as she sat up. "Jackson, I..."

He pulled her back to him to remind himself of dreams that almost came true, and silenced her with a final kiss. He then drew back and brought them both back to reality. "Don't start anything you can't finish, Alex. I know you said I was part of a summer dream, but I'm hoping you know there's more to it than that."

Looking to her hands, now drawing figures in the dirt, she remembered how he'd looked when she'd told him that first kiss was nice but going nowhere. She'd been struggling for control then, but now it didn't seem to matter. She looked up to him, sitting in the dirt beside her, his jeaned legs touching hers, surrounding her like his heart surrounded her soul.

"I always finish what I start."

"Including engagements, because, Alex, I'm not going to romance another man's woman. I'm not that kind, and I'm willing to bet you're not either."

"No," she said, wrapping her arms around his neck. "I'm not," she said, knowing this was where she wanted to be and growing more determined with each word. "Paul and I—"

She was stopped cold by the instant anger in his eyes and felt compelled to increase her hold on his neck. He broke her grip and set her hands in her lap.

"We talked."

He brought one foot under him and propped an elbow on his knee. "And?"

"And I told him we were no longer engaged; we both knew it was largely a business relationship from the beginning and…" She faltered when the reality of what she was about to say hit her. She cleared her throat but couldn't look at him for fear of seeing rejection in his eyes. "And..." She suddenly took refuge in Alexandria. "I have reassessed my priorities and found something…" she had to clear her throat again to finish. "*Someone*, who"—she looked directly into his delicious brown eyes and her courage was renewed—"someone who frightens me a little, but excites me like nothing I've ever experienced before."

"Alex," he said as he stood, his voice husky and soft, "don't do this to me. I can't kiss you again only to have you run away. I keep trying to forget the two days you just spent with your fiancé, and I'm no fool."

She shook her head. "I told you, we're not engaged anymore."

He laughed. "And realistically, you'll be gone in a week or so, and I'll just be a memory."

"No, Jackson."

"No, what? You won't be gone in a week or I won't even be a memory?"

She wasn't sure how to answer, so she didn't.

"I'll put our horses up. You stay here or, better yet, go to the house and take a good hot shower. That'll help take some of the soreness out." He turned and walked away.

CHAPTER 7

*M**emory*...the melancholy words to the Broadway song, "Noise from traffic nearby, unseen people talking, the clatter of dishes from somewhere below, sounds she never heard before," drifted through Alexandria's mind. She tried not to imagine Jackson ever being a mere memory, but knew that was what loomed ahead if she couldn't find a way to talk to him. His back to her, every step he took as he walked across the arena and away from her tore a little more from her heart, drove another nail in the door closing their relationship.

Her persuasive talents were known from one end of the country to the other and in many circles in Europe; why, then, was it so impossible to express herself to Jackson? Why did she choke up like a junior partner? Standing, alone, frustrated, and suddenly feeling cold and numb, she hid her face with both hands while she tried to think. *Take Jackson's advice.* She wiped away dirt and sticky sweat from her cheeks and forehead, then continued on to rake her fingers through her hair. The biggest challenge of her life had just walked away and she was powerless to stop him. Maybe a shower would cleanse body and soul.

Half an hour later, the pounding hot water had worked its magic on her stiffening muscles, but left her soul still wanting. Wanting Jackson. Wanting his arms around her and his lips on hers. Wanting a meeting of minds and hearts that would satisfy them both. She curled in his chair by the window and looked toward the barn where he was. His house was silent. She leaned her head back and closed her eyes, drank in the smell of *his* house and memorized the feel of it. She wished the simple mobile home could tell her what words to use to give her a place inside his heart.

She had never felt the pull of family, but this simple place felt like it held the key to all that was missing. Kids giggling and shouting, running through the sprinklers on a hot day; a mother and father settling in together on a rainy day and wondering how they were going to entertain their brood; sweet, meaningful smiles between a man and a woman.

A hawk flying overhead called out to its partner in a shrill shriek, and instantly her thoughts turned toward the barn. She wished she could be a mouse, hidden from sight but able to see and hear everything Jackson did, but quickly the idea failed. She didn't want to be an outsider. She didn't want vicarious thrills, she wanted the real thing, she wanted Jackson. Had she known that he fared no better than she at the moment, that his confusion was just as complete as hers, she might have seen some glimmer of hope.

His thoughts practically mirrored hers, his frustration was as hers, his yearnings were the same. He'd never been an eloquent speaker, but Jackson usually knew what he wanted and had little trouble getting it—until Alexandria Payne stepped into his life. Like a robot, he put both his horses up, turned them out, and began with Alexandria's mount. He dropped the breast collar and cinch and was about to pull the saddle when he stopped. Gently he ran his fingers over the place her leg had been and where she had been sitting.

The leather was cold, but he swore he felt heat. She was the most apt student he'd ever trained and had enough talent to do whatever she pleased with a horse. Jackson smiled and thought to himself that it wasn't only horses she mesmerized; she'd worked him into a lather like an over-eager colt and left him begging for more. He drummed his fingers on the seat for an instant, then slapped the saddle and pulled it off to put it away, like he wanted to put thoughts of her away.

He needed to ride one more horse, but knew better than to work when his mind was not focused on business. The turbulence called Alexandria thinned his patience, piqued his temper without cause, and flawed his strategy.

Habit took over chores and he worked absently, quickly, efficiently at first. Little by little, he slowed as his mind centered on Alexandria. What would happen when he went back to the house? Would she be angry or meek? Could he take her in his arms or would he pretend he wasn't on fire for her?

The more he tried to predict the outcome, the less he hurried. The more he realized he had no idea what would come, the more intrigued he was with the woman who still had not let her hair down, whose mouth cried out to be kissed and whose body tempted even a saint. This was the point, total frustration, where he usually decided to counsel with Joker. His friend always listened and never gave bad advice. He picked up a brush, took an apple from the bag, and went to the pen behind the barn.

"I think you like her too," he told the old horse who nuzzled him for more. "She is gentle and generous—you know she's responsible for the apple." He brushed for several minutes, but found no answer to the problem she posed. "I suppose you're being close-mouthed for a reason. Must be that I have to figure this one out for myself. Well," he stroked the wise old campaigner, "guess I'd better go face my dragon and find out if I'm smart enough to slay it."

He strolled to the tack room, replaced the brushes, and began to wipe down the equipment they'd just used. As he worked, the romantic in him wanted to step boldly forward, take her into his arms, kiss her until she was senseless with passion, then sweep her into *his* bedroom and make her forever, indelibly his.

Of course, his next thought was that the night would be a wild one. Alex was no ordinary woman. Finished cleaning, he stopped, leaned against the tack room doorjamb, crossed his arms, and sighed. He could think of worse ways to go, but he would much rather have her wanting him as much as he wanted her.

But it was clear she didn't want him. She'd just spent two days and a night with her fiancé, and whether or not it was the perfect relationship, he knew better than to step in where he wasn't wanted. He pushed off the door, closed it, and took a deep breath. Logically, there was nothing more to do here, unless he started on odd jobs that had already been put off and could reasonably wait even longer. It was his house. She was his guest. He should have no dread of going home, but as he began the long walk up the hill, the part of him she stirred was not convinced.

Was she watching?

Would she be waiting in the living room for him or would she be naked in his shower?

Hating himself for indecision and for wanting something that might never be his, he trudged on. Nothing was certain, he thought as he tried to put determination in his pace. About halfway there, he gave up. It felt like there was more swagger and false bravado in his walk than real courage, and Jackson was no fool. It was senseless to try to be something he wasn't. And what he was was a man reeling in frustration, confused by his inability to get what he wanted…right now.

The hike up the driveway had never seemed so long or so difficult. He had no idea what he was going to say, but his plan was to let her begin. He stepped on the front deck, the sound of his feet a surreal sound to him. The screen door squeaked for the first time ever as he opened it, announcing his arrival. He stepped inside and saw her in his chair; instantly he knew she had been watching. The knowledge warmed him. He let go of the screen. It slapped behind him, but he heard nothing because she was silent. Slowly he came to her.

She smiled.

Jackson pulled the leather ottoman to her feet, swung his leg over and straddled it.

"Appears we got some talking to do."

Still curled up, like a small child, she nodded. A single tear slipped from the corner of one eye, and he saw a vulnerable woman waiting for love, rather than a corporate giant. Jackson reached out to her, wiping the tear from her cheek with his thumb. Suddenly he knew where to start. "I guess it's time to lay it all on the line and speak nothing but the truth."

He watched her carefully as he spoke, and although the sound of his raspy whisper seemed to calm her, fear still glistened in her eyes. It hurt to think he was the cause. He took one of her hands in his.

"I've always been pretty sure where I was going and what I wanted. Hell, even as a snot-nosed kid, I knew I wasn't going to be happy with an eight-to-five job in some stuffy building. I also knew that I was happy being alone. Except for Everett, there wasn't a soul I cared for or needed, until I met you…" He played with the end of her braided hair and focused on it for a moment before fixing his gaze on her face. "I've had to rethink things that have been second nature to me for a long time."

It was a simple declaration. In his own way, Jackson was allowing her to see inside him, to know as much about the man, perhaps, as he knew about himself. Alexandria was moved by it and prayed for God to give her the wisdom and patience to listen and learn—something she'd never seen the need for until now.

Smiling through the tears, she gave him all the encouragement she knew how.

He took both her trembling hands in his, sharing the heat and intensity of the moment. "I guess what I'm trying to get to is that when I have trouble with a horse or anything else, I try to face it and be honest with myself about the problem. For the last month, Alex, I've been having a hell of a time dealing with you, and it's because I haven't had the guts to face the problem head-on."

Alexandria suddenly found the air stifling, and the simple act of breathing had become almost impossible. Jackson Morgan had enough of her. She was the cause of too many problems. He was ready to be rid of her. What began as a business deal was going to end as a business deal.

It wasn't fair, her heart cried out. Just as she found love, it was disappearing. The one thing that could make her life truly a success was slipping through her fingers and evaporating before her eyes.

"I'm sorry—" she began as more tears fell. "I never meant to be such a—"

"No, no." He pulled her toward him, nervous laughter soothing them both. "I'm not sorry for a minute that I met you, and I hope the feeling's mutual. What we gotta do is face the fact that there might be something between us that goes further than a good cut or a nice turn. We need to decide what that is." His eyes grew dark with emotion and his voice deepened. "I don't think I can live without finding what's there, and I think you agree. We've both been playing games with each other and it's time we quit."

She sniffed, marveling how he had made sense out of chaos when she had failed. "Yes, yes to everything." She forced a smile again. "I guess I'm not as good at being just plain Alex as I am at being Alexandria, but I'm willing to try."

"You *are* Alex." He gently pulled her onto his lap. "Your nose is a little pink from the sun, your jeans are pressed and neat in the morning but dusted with dirt around the bottom after working stock all day. You are my Alex." He reached for her thick blonde braid. "Do you know you've been here nearly a month, and I've never seen your hair free except for the day Paul was here? My Alex wears it just like you do when she rides, but at home, when she wants to be soft, she lets it fall." He unwound the rubber band and then his fingers combed through her golden tresses, leaving wide, luxurious curls falling around her shoulders.

"Some mornings, when we're up early and the sun is just coming up, your hair looks like spun gold."

His touch was careful but deliberate, and Alexandria felt the power of his determination meet and blend with her own. Nestled in his lap, she was warmed by his thighs alongside hers and by the closeness of his chest to her back.

"It's been all I could do to leave your hair alone," he continued to stroke it as he spoke, "not to mention all the times I had the urge to do this..." He nuzzled her neck, parting the hair to allow himself clear access.

Chills ran through Alexandria and she itched to return caress for caress, but he held her close so the only thing she could do was lean into him. Finally, her pulse racing, her breath ragged, he put his arms around her, content to hold her, content to be together at last. Even after a hard day in the saddle, she smelled like wild honeysuckle.

"Jackson?"

"Yes."

She turned to face him, reluctant to break his hold, but intent upon clearing the way for them. "Jackson, I'm not good at things like this. I've got no idea where we're going, but like you, I need to know."

"I guess curiosity might kill us two cats." He leaned forward and brushed a light kiss on her lips. "But I suspect we might have a darn good time researching the subject."

Jackson stood, taking Alex with him. He gathered her closer and delivered a quick kiss to her forehead.

Her legs felt like jelly, and she silently thanked God they were going to have a second chance. Releasing her, Jackson stretched tall as if he were a man awakened from a long slumber. "I'm sorry you fell."

Mention of the accident suddenly brought her aching muscles to mind. "It wasn't your fault." She smiled, tossing her hair back at the same time. "I was getting kind of cocky and it taught me a lesson."

"Are you pretty sore?" His concerned tone carried through in his expression, but he quickly followed up with a smile.

"Not sore enough to miss practice tomorrow. I seem to remember you betting you'd score higher than me."

"I did?" His face brightened with humor and suddenly all was well.

She put her hands on her hips and challenged him in fun. "You did, and I intend to hold you to it."

Jackson nodded in appreciation of her spunk. The possibility of her scoring higher than him in a novice horse class was a distinct possibility and should have scared him a little, but it didn't. He knew if he were to be beaten, she'd do it fair and square. He also knew that he wanted success for her as much or more than he wanted success for himself. Tough as nails, gentle as the wind, his Alex stood before him, and there was nothing he could refuse her.

After a simple dinner, Jackson and Alexandria decided to watch the sunset from the lawn in back of the house. He suggested the rustic log-and-wagon-wheel swing, but she opted for the grass itself, which was a good deal softer than the board seat.

A frown darkened his face, like a cloud crossing the sunlit hills as he settled in the grass. "I am sorry about getting after you so bad this afternoon. You're a natural at cutting and I—" He looked at her as she nestled beside him and realized he was on his way to another lie. The real issue hadn't anything to do with cutting or horses. He'd promised to be truthful and he owed himself, as well as her, nothing less.

"Nope," he forced a correction. "That's got little or nothing to do with what happened today. Not that you aren't doing great, but—" He cleared his throat, then stopped.

The pause nearly killed Alexandria. She imagined all kinds of reasons for his impatience ranging from her stupidity to his tiring of her. She waited, frozen, unable to look at him, unable to breathe.

He began slowly, carefully, watching her, recognizing how still she was and praying he could find the words to melt the brittle veneer she hid behind. "After that first kiss, you made it clear where I stand, and I know I'm the one who's stepping into territory I have no right to be in, but you're like a horn fly that won't go away. The thought of you and him buzzed around my head until I thought I was going to go crazy." Tight and tense, he feared the worst, and his plea tumbled out like grain spilling from a torn bag. "The more I swatted at it the faster it buzzed, and by the time you finally got back, I had no idea how to deal with it." The words weren't right, he felt like a horse stumbling through a rock creek bed. "I'll apologize now, for the liberties I've taken by trying to explain, but it doesn't change the fact that I'm having a helluva time trying to forget you and him together."

Alex felt afraid and happy all at once. She wasn't the only one who had been fighting a feeling that was as mysterious as it was intriguing. They were seated close, almost face-to-face, and she knew it was her turn to speak, to tell him he wasn't out of line, to confess all. She picked a blade of grass and twirled it between her thumb and forefinger while she thought how she would begin.

"It wasn't like that," she whispered. "He had business to discuss and there were papers to sign, but," she looked from the grass to him, "I also had something to discuss, and I went with him so we'd have no interruptions."

"Carmel?"

"How do you know we went to Carmel?" she asked cautiously.

"Paul called, just to let me know where you could be reached if necessary," Jackson said flatly.

"Oh." She returned her focus to the grass, aware of Paul's intent, but not surprised—it was the way they worked. He started to say something, but she gently silenced him with her fingers as she continued. "It was never a real engagement. It just happened because neither of us had time for anyone else and because it seemed prudent at the time. It was more a business deal than not, and right now, I realize that it was a cheap trick to avoid anything more real."

Jackson was silent, almost brooding.

"You have to understand there wasn't much feeling associated with it. I didn't understand that myself until I found out… until I met someone who made me feel."

He leaned back, supported by one elbow, and toyed with the grass. Alexandria felt that companionable feeling slipping away and was afraid what progress they'd made had been destroyed. She came to her knees and leaned forward, trying to close the space. "I told him—"

Swiftly he pulled her down and to him, then rolled, pinning her beneath him. "I don't want to hear what you told him. All I want to hear is that he doesn't matter anymore. I want the chance to court you like a gentleman and love you like a mad man."

Her body burned where his lay across hers, and the fire spread inside and out. She would have agreed to anything just to keep him near. "Jackson Morgan, I've never met anyone like you. No one else matters—no one but you."

Jackson's body was as ready as his mind to taste again what he'd hungered for so long. Pressing himself slowly against her, his lips finally met hers. The kiss was deep and long lasting, a prelude to what was to follow. Neither he nor she wanted to rush.

Alex savored him like a connoisseur savors a fine wine, tasting, smelling, and allowing him to swirl around in her mind until she was dizzy with him. She clung to him, like a leaf clings to its stem for life. The setting sun cast a golden glow upon them and the cool grass pillowed them as they rolled, each wanting and wishing for the power that would make them one.

Jackson scattered kisses over her neck, sending shivers of joy through her. Throwing caution to the delicate evening breeze, he found the top button on her blouse and unbuttoned it, chasing his handiwork with kisses where her shoulder began. She was warm and soft, and the hint of honeysuckle was as intoxicating as the strongest opiate. He'd dreamed of this moment a thousand times each night and thought he knew what euphoria it would produce, but realized he'd been wrong. Nothing his mind could conjure matched the powerful feelings he had as his body lay beside hers and his arms held her tight.

"Where have you been all my life," he said, his voice husky and passion ravaged. "I've wasted a lot of time thinking I was above needing someone."

"I don't even want to think about the time we've wasted. We're here, and we finally found each other." His body was warm and inviting as he pressed to her. Alex was sure she'd been shot with electricity. Her whole being tingled and suddenly there was no time to tarry. "Make love to me, Jackson. I don't think I can live without you closer to me now. I need you, I love you."

Breathless, all he heard was her declaration of love. "Is that where we are? Is this crazy obsession really love?"

She slowed her pursuit of him, almost the same time he hesitated, the reality of what they were saying hitting them both.

He rolled to his back and gazed toward the starry heaven.

Alex laid her head on the grass carpet and smiled. "I can't speak for you, but I honestly think I'm in love with you, Jackson. Since the first day I came to you, there's been that same horn fly bugging me. I tried to ignore it, and I tried to explain it away, but

I could never quite forget the way your voice sounds or the gentleness and thrill of your touch or"—she laughed—"the fact that you're a better cook than I am."

He reached for her hand and held it tight. "I love you too, Alex."

She stopped. "You don't have to say it just because I did."

He rolled to face her. "I'm not. You make me feel alive and itchy all over."

"Poison oak would do the same thing."

"You're definitely under my skin, like poison oak, but I hope the feeling is going to last a lot longer." He focused on her face, a healthy tan from the sun, cheeks pink from body heat, and lips red from meeting his. "I want this to last forever."

"Forever would be nice."

"I have to have forever. I can't—"

"You have to trust me," she whispered. "You have to trust us. I'm a beginner at this too, and I know we have to be sure, but I know how I've felt up till now, and there's never been anything close to you, Jackson. I know my heart."

"A kiss to seal the deal?"

She wound her arms around his neck and drew him closer. "More than one would make it an iron-clad contract."

Darkness crept over them as each one bargained for the other's heart. Some moments were frantic as the beginning had been, but most were slow and gentle, the way a man woos a woman he cares for deeply and the way a woman builds and binds a man's mind and body.

Neither knew how long they had been in each other's arms, but when each was satisfied just to lie in the other's embrace, time resurfaced.

"We need to be up early," he said lazily, the purple haze of honeysuckle still lingering over him. He caressed her hair, silvery and alive in the moonlight as she rested her head on his chest.

"I know. Will you come to bed with me?" She felt rather than heard him laugh. "What? Is that funny?"

"No. It's just that earlier tonight, I thought maybe the way to win you was the Rhett Butler approach. I considered marching up to you and carrying you to *my* bed and ravishing you until you gave in."

"You could still do it." His chest rose and fell and she ran her hand across it lovingly.

"Nope. This battle has been won with remarkably few casualties, and I think I'm happy to be on the couch." She tried to raise her head in protest, but he held her close. "Neither of us is going anywhere and I, for one, am content to know there will be a tomorrow for us. We have lots to learn about each other before we share a bed."

Alex knew he was right. Finding a soul mate after years of searching was enough for one night. Unlike Scarlett, she didn't have to worry about tomorrow.

Between packing for Temecula and practice, the next day was busy and long. Alex rode as many horses as she could, warming up some for Jackson and working Hattie especially hard. Most of the time, Jackson was patient and happy with her work, but he purposely had her ride the lazy roan as well as another gelding, which challenged her ability.

Jackson watched Alex ride and marveled at how easily she sat a working horse and how her energy seemed to flow from her to the animal. It was as if the tension between them had evaporated, leaving her more focused and adept than ever. She was a natural, and it pleased him to be part of the awakening of such a talent.

Later that afternoon, Everett called and Jackson expounded upon the subject of his favorite student. "You should see her, Ev; she has come a long way in a month. Of course, you didn't see her in the very beginning, when she didn't know long from short, deep from shallow, or a high score from a hot quit."

"Sounds like you're her promoter, son. What's been going on between the long and the short go-rounds?"

Hesitation on the other end worried Everett. "You're not getting in too deep with the lady from the big city, are you?"

"No. Not too deep. I think she's the one, Ev, and we've finally come to an understanding about each other. I like her. I like her a lot, and if you hang around long enough, you might get to be best man."

"You're falling fast, Jackson. When I was out there, I was worried about where that cute face and saucy little butt was leadin' you. Don't suppose I could interest you in taking more time?"

"Ev. I'm thirty-six years old. You always said I'd find someone who would make me want to settle down and have kids. You like her. I know you do, otherwise you'd have said so."

"Arguin' with you is like tryin' to find hair on a frog, as usual. I guess there's nothin' to say but go for it. Jist take it from an old man and go slow. If she's the one, she'll be there tomorrow."

Jackson couldn't help but wish Everett had been in on their "tomorrow" conversation. Surely he'd feel more at ease about Alex if he'd heard her view on tomorrow. When he hung up, Ev had hinted that he might show up at Temecula, and Jackson hoped then he and Alexandria would have the chance to talk more. Everett was the only father he'd ever really known, and no matter what else was said, it mattered to him what Everett thought.

Later that same day, after dinner, he and Alex were making final plans for the trip to Temecula. Juan was going to take care of the ranch, but between hauling horses, making motel and boarding arrangements, and packing everything, the list grew longer and longer. Alex sat on the couch finishing up laundry (she had been given explicit instructions on how not to shrink anything) and Jackson was making the final phone calls.

Alex was almost too excited to be content folding clothes; this was a big show, with tough competition and prestige.

She'd been to events sanctioned by the National Cutting Horse Association with Jackson before, but this was a money-added show that attracted all the right people. Most of the big Texas trainers would be there, as well as many celebrity contestants like Joe Montana and Christie Brinkley.

Suddenly she clutched the T-shirt she was folding to her chest. What was wrong with her? Her month was almost up. Everett might be there, and she was supposed to deliver. She'd promised Paul over and over she had things under control, but now for the first time, she realized that more had changed than her feelings for Jackson.

She turned around toward the hallway and the open door to his office. His voice was clear as a bell as he spoke to the motel clerk and confirmed the reservations for their room. *Room. Singular, not plural.* A sick, weak feeling hit her in the pit of her stomach and she sat back, still holding Jackson's shirt close. She brought it up to her face, closed her eyes, and inhaled. Even freshly washed, it smelled of liniment and saddle soap—just like Jackson. How was she going to balance what was left of her business life with what was to be of her personal one?

She hadn't spoken to Paul since her return from Carmel. It was as if her life had begun all over, and her responsibility to APM had been forgotten like a cloud on a sunny day.

"Done deal." Jackson surprised her as his arms closed around her in a full-on hug. "I've made my last phone call." He moved around to her side, pushed the pile of clean clothes away, and sat beside her on the couch. "All we have to do is pack our bags and we're off bright and early tomorrow morning."

"I don't know how bright I'll be at three thirty a.m.," she shook out the shirt and hurriedly folded it, "but, yes, we'll be on our way."

He leaned back, watching her fold. His gaze was hot upon her and Alex suddenly stopped and turned to him, her expression sober. "I love you, Jackson."

Smiling, he opened his arms and invited her to come to him. Alex welcomed his strong hands as they gathered her up and held her tight.

She had always been a smart and resourceful person. There had to be a way to deal with this problem, and she was sure she could find a solution that was acceptable to all involved. All her life, she had been a problem solver and all her life, she had triumphed over the odds. There was no reason to think she would fail now, especially when so much was at stake.

Alexandria settled into Jackson's arms. She felt safe and loved. Snuggling closer she let herself be taken away to a place where there was no conflict and no treachery.

"Remember that bet that you'd score higher than me?" he said.

"Sure. I'm gonna give it my best shot, but what kind of chance does the pupil have against the pro?" she teased.

"Well, if you rode that new little palomino gelding for me in the two-thousand limit class, you'd have a great chance."

The palomino had been getting better and better every day. He was still green, but when she had warmed him up for Jackson, she knew they had clicked. Apparently Jackson knew it too.

"You'd let me ride him?"

"Sure. He's owned by a woman and will be shown by a woman. There's no reason you shouldn't take him in Temecula. I have two other horses to ride in that class and you'll be helping me."

She sat up, eager to ride the flashy little horse. "Well, OK then. You've got yourself a rider."

The following day, excitement fueled plenty of verbal exchange for the first third of the trip, but conversation on the road died down afterwards; one hour wore on into the next. Silence had its place, though, and both Alex and Jackson settled into a comfortable kind of relaxation that comes with confidence and familiarity. She sat next to him, enjoying the warmth of his leg beside hers and relishing the moments when he rested his hand on her thigh.

As Jackson drove down Interstate 5, Alex watched miles and miles of flat, uninspiring farmland fly by. A nagging comparison between the acreage and her life wormed its way into her mind; desolate, dry, and separated from the rest of the world, it needed only care and a little nourishment to become the rich agricultural land that provided food for California and many other states. Similarly, her life up to now had been dry and semi-isolated, with only a veneer of productivity. In reality, what had she ever produced? Money? Ill will? Who would ever know how many dollars she earned fifty years from now, and for that matter, who would care?

She looked to Jackson. He was nourishment for her soul. He had given her a new life. A cold shiver ran through her; what might be emerging between them was the most frightening, abstract thing she'd ever dealt with in all her years of runaway successes. Real relationships, love, children—time was running out on her ability to become part of these incredible waves of human care and kindness, and perhaps Jackson had been sent by fate to save her from withering away in a lonely excuse for life. It struck her again that time was running out in a number of ways, but the most unnerving for her was the fact that in a few hours she and Jackson would enter a motel room and then look at each other, wondering what the other was thinking. He'd proven he was capable of total honesty, but was she?

Almost fifteen hours later, she and Jackson pulled into the motel after dropping off horses and trailer at the stable. Jackson had gone to the office, so she hadn't a clue how he had explained the two of them. It didn't matter; the end result was that they were going to spend their first night together.

He came through the glass door, tossing keys in one hand, whistling. He seemed so happy, so untroubled by what was becoming a huge problem in her mind. Minute after minute ticked away and with each one her apprehension grew.

"Number 108 and 109, connecting," he said as he hopped in beside her and started the engine. "Let's get the rest of this stuff unloaded and go to dinner. I'm as hungry as a bum looking in a deli window."

"Me too," Alex seconded, a bit too quickly. "I mean, I'm pretty hungry," she corrected, suddenly feeling self-conscious. "How about eating before we go to our rooms?"

"Fine with me, we'll just stow our bags in the cab while we eat. How about that coffee shop we passed on the way in." He looked to her as he shifted into drive. "Or would you like to go someplace fancier?"

"Coffee shop is fine," she said, again a bit too eagerly. He must have sensed something in either her voice or her body language since he stopped, looked at her, and smiled.

"The rooms are connecting, only because that is what they had left," he said.

Alex blew out a long breath as she took his arm and hugged it like a lifeline. "Good, I mean, well, we both need to get a good night's rest. I don't mind telling you I am a little nervous."

"Nothing to worry about," he said as he held the door to the coffee shop open for her. "You have a good horse, and you are entered in a class that you have a good chance of winning." He stopped her in the entry, took her by the shoulders, and looked her straight in the eye. "You *have* done your homework. Stop worrying."

She smiled and wondered if he could see in her eyes that the competition was only a small part of her concern. All those positive things she'd thought earlier about being rescued from a dry life of business seemed to have lost their validity. That life had been quite free of doubt and indecision and was certainly a lot easier on her ego than the roller coaster she rode now.

The meal they shared and the short walk back to the motel passed so quickly that Alexandria hardly remembered a single moment. She couldn't have repeated a word of their conversation or related whether she had chicken or beef. It seemed that only minutes had passed from the time Jackson came from the office to the time she found herself behind a closed motel door face-to-face with the most virile, powerful man she had ever known.

He set her last bag on the folding stand. In his other hand, he carried his ditty bag with his personal items. She looked quickly at it and imagined him casually putting it in her bathroom. The room suddenly seemed tiny and stuffy.

"Alex?" his voice echoed softly in her mind. She saw nothing but concern in his face.

He stuffed one hand in his pocket and stood hipshot with one knee relaxed while he looked to the floor. He sighed, and she knew he'd not been as carefree as he appeared. For an eternity there was no sound but that of a distant child's mournful wail and a car door slamming.

She turned away from him so that he might not see the yearning in her eyes. Why was she having such a hard time loving the man who had changed her life?

Silently he moved up behind her, took her by the shoulders, and turned her to face him. "Honestly, between you and me, I'm more than a little bit nervous too. I thought this night would be no big deal. There were other rooms available, but I…that is, I thought I would make it easier for us to be together." Jackson let a huge sigh free and she saw his body relax. "I've slept with women before and I've had no complaints, but this time *is* different. I love you, Alex. This is more important than anything I've done before."

Relief produced a single tear that slid from the corner of her eye and bounced along her cheek. "I can't believe I'm crying again. How do you know the right thing to say every time I'm speechless?" She put her arms around his narrow waist and hugged him to her, resting her face against his broad chest. "How am I ever going to be there for you, the way you are for me?"

Jackson wrapped one arm around her neck, bringing her closer, and caressed her cheek with the other. "Let your hair down, Rapunzel, and let me rescue you from yourself. You worry too much."

Alex pushed away far enough to remove the clip that kept her hair wound tight. Like molten gold, Jackson watched her hair fall around her face and shoulders. Everything about her was amazing; everything about her pleased him. He held her by the waist, forcing her hips and legs to stay pressed against his as she leaned back.

She smiled as she tossed her head, then leaned closer to him. Her breath was warm against his neck as she wiggled, snuggling closer, driving his body and mind crazy with desire.

"I don't want to rush you, but if you continue to rub all over me like this, I'm not going to—"

"I'm not asking you to stop, Jackson. We've stopped before and I spent the rest of the night wishing we hadn't." She ran her fingers through his hair and he felt control slipping away.

"I've made a few real mistakes in my life, and all I can think of now is that I damn sure don't want to make a mistake this time."

Slowly she pulled back and toyed with the buttons on his shirt, "If you're talking about 'us' being a mistake, we'd better stop, but if you're talking about rushing into a relationship, then listen to me. If we just let things proceed at their own pace and don't try to arrange it one way or the other, we'll be fine. I want to be as close to you as I can get, and I'm not a baby, Jackson. I know what I'm doing." She drew closer and nibbled at his ear. "And I know I want you."

He groaned and wrapped his arms around her, lifting her off the floor. "Then let 'er rip." He swung her around and around, lavishing kisses on her ear and neck as he went. The last time around, he reached for her legs and picked her up and carried her to the bed where he laid her carefully and followed her down.

Alex pulled Jackson's shoulders to her, and the feel of his hard, muscled body drove her to the peak of her imagination. She suddenly sat straight up, leaving him surprised and lost.

"What's wrong?" he whispered, already short of breath.

"Nothing." She smoothed his hair where she had ruffled it. "Nothing at all." The sparkle in her eyes dared him to come closer. His smile answered as he leaned to her.

It was a slow dance, done to the music of love, choreography perfected by hundreds of thousands of years of men and women craving passion, wanting each other. Perfection was the meeting of minds and bodies in an ageless ritual, and Jackson and Alexandria were lost in each other, mindless of any concern, above the mundane problems of the day, of the world.

It was the way nature intended it to be. One man, one woman. Bound together by the sense that each would cease to live without the other. Alexandria knew she would never be complete again without him, and the tender, loving way his body answered hers told her she was part of him forever.

Alex was on the edge and knew Jackson was too, when he suddenly forced himself away. Breathless, all he said was "Enough."

Her mind screamed that it wasn't enough, that she needed more, and she wiggled closer to retrieve the next kiss.

"Alex. We need to stop."

"I'll get plenty of sleep later."

"No." He sat up, leaving her still on the bed. "I want you more than anything else in the world, but not here. Not in a motel, not in a bed that belongs to someone else."

She sat up, smoothing her hair back from her face. "Are you sure?"

He stood. "Never been more sure of anything in my life. You belong in my bed for the first time, and I want it to be more than a coffee shop evening." He knelt before her and took her hand. "I know you've been wined and dined in places I've never even dreamed of, but I want to give you romance. I want to hear you sigh and smile like a child who sees what she wants under the Christmas tree and who knows that Santa Claus does exist. I want to make you forget everything but me."

"Are you for real?" was all Alex could think of to say. "I have never felt so loved, so special. I couldn't explain how wonderful I feel right now if I tried, Jackson. You've said everything a woman wants to hear, and it was all sincere. I can't believe I have found you." She whispered, "You're not gay, are you?"

He stood and for a moment she thought she'd made him angry. "No. I'm damn sure not gay. I'm in love with you, Alexandria Payne."

She stood and tiptoed to reach his lips. "Then you'd better leave now, before we both lose control. I'm going to score higher than you do day after tomorrow and you'd better be ready to pay off."

When morning came, Jackson thought he would be exhausted by hours of lying awake, imagining Alex asleep in the next room, but he woke fresher and more alive than ever. He peeked through the connecting door and saw Alex was still asleep. He showered, and when he was ready to go feed, he couldn't bear to disturb her. She slept like an angel. He laughed at himself. She *was* an angel, and she was his; he'd never been more satisfied with life.

He scribbled a note to her telling her he'd be back to take her for breakfast after he checked and fed the horses. As soon as he closed the door, he wanted to reopen it and look once more, but he thought it might wake her and resisted the urge. It was a little hard to believe that he had found her. She'd been hiding from him in a place he'd never thought to look, and by some freak coincidence, she'd come to him. It didn't matter how she'd come, he wasn't going to look a gift horse, so to speak, in the mouth. She was here, and he was ready to do whatever it took to keep her.

CHAPTER 8

Alex had just put coffee in the little pot provided by the motel when there was a knock. Thinking it could be only Jackson, she ran to open the door. "Forget your key—"

"Hello, little darlin'." Everett stood, hat in hand, smiling.

"Well, hello. Come in, Jackson will be back any minute. In fact, I thought it was him when you knocked."

Everett walked into the room stepping as slow as his Texas drawl. Alex sensed something was awry. "Can I get you…coffee, water, soda?"

He turned, running his fingers around the brim of his hat, like a man fingering the trigger. "Make your move," he said simply, no humor, no good will apparent on his face or in his eyes.

"I beg your pardon?"

He stood tall and his voice hardened. "I said. Make your move. You've set everything up for the kill, and I'm waiting to hear your offer."

Alex felt her face getting hot and red, something that would have never happened a month ago when she would have been able to run a good bluff rather than admit the truth. "Rawlins Shipping."

"Among other things, I suppose. Your 'friend' Paul Maitland just bought up the mortgage on Jackson's place, and I can see that sooner or later, you'll use your influence on Jackson to get Rawlins or anything else you want."

"Paul bought the mortgage on—"

"Don't pretend you're surprised. You're a little more crafty than I thought, but I guess I was guilty of underestimating you from the beginning."

Alex backed away and sat on the bed. No wonder Paul had been so quiet lately. He'd been planning and making moves on his own. She looked to Everett and realized the direct approach was the only thing that would work now. "When did you know who I was?"

He threw his hat on the dresser and stared at her like she was a sidewinder. "When Jackson told me about his new, too-good-to-refuse deal, I got suspicious and decided to see just who his golden goose was. I hadn't put the name with APM then, but it sure wasn't a stretch to see what you were up to. I just didn't think Jackson would fall for you and give you an extra bargaining tool."

She stood, ready to argue her case. "You have it all wrong. When I came here, I had no idea that you even knew Jackson. I admit I wanted to learn how to cut in order to get close to you, but I never knew Jackson would be a part of that."

"And I think you're lying. You and Paul are much too shrewd for things like this to fall coincidentally."

"You are so wrong," she pleaded, her face blanching.

"I don't think so." He began pacing. "What I'm here for now is to make things right. I thought you'd have about as much chance with Jackson as a hen at a mass meeting of coyotes, but I guess I was wrong. Now all I want is to get him away from you so he can forget everything about you, so he can live his life without having his heart ripped out."

Alex tried to stand her ground although her stomach felt as if someone had kicked her. "I'd never hurt Jackson," she whispered.

"Of course you wouldn't. That's why you bought his mortgage and why you're going to call it if I don't sell Rawlins." He continued to stroll back and forth as if she were not standing in his path. "I know your type. You're a barracuda; part of the fun of winning is tearing apart your victim. Jackson met someone like you a while ago, and he's still recovering. But," he stopped suddenly and directed a cold, heartless stare at her, "of course you knew that before you got here. You knew he'd be hungry for money. Hell"—he threw his arms up—"you even knew exactly how much to offer."

"What are you talking about?" she said, truly worried and feeling the walls closing in around her.

"OK. I guess I'll play along with you. Jackson used to do very well giving lessons to a number of people. One of which was a woman much like yourself, who thought winning was the most important thing." He turned his back on Alexandria, as if he could no longer look at her. "She was a non-pro, who was limited to riding her own horse, and when it came to a big money prize, she drugged her horse. Well, the National Cutting Horse Association did random testing and happened to pick her horse. Not only did it come up dirty, but it was a ringer, not even her horse. Jackson, her trainer, got fined and suspended, which I'm sure you had no trouble finding out. Then she proceeded to attack everyone, from the judges to Jackson, and when he didn't stand up for her, she sued him. It cost him everything he had saved for the ten-thousand-dollar balloon payment on his place, and the suspension made sure he had no way to earn it back in time—no way but your very convenient offer. I tried to loan him money, but he wouldn't have it. It's important to him that he's his own man, you know."

Alex's heart ached for Jackson; as honest as the day was long, he'd been vandalized. She knew without a doubt that what Everett said had happened precisely the way he explained, but she saw too clearly how the case against her was becoming iron-clad. "You have to believe me...I didn't know. I just told Hesperia to find me the best trainer. *I didn't know.*"

Her plea was unanswered; he continued as if she'd said nothing. "Well, you have all the cards. Your competitive edge is such that you ought to hand out Band-Aids to your business associates. But"—he turned and captured her in his hateful glare—"Jackson is a son to me. I'm not going to allow you to make him suffer. Rawlins is yours, but let's make it a sporting deal, something a woman like you can brag about at the next corporate meeting. I heard you bet Jackson you'd beat him this weekend. I'll sweeten the pot. You beat him and I'll sell you Rawlins for whatever price you name."

She stood, her silence filling the room along with James Everett Covington's contempt for her. How could she convince him she was not the conniving hussy he thought her to be? She used to be, but she honestly knew she didn't have the stomach for it now. Tears of despair welled in her eyes.

"Not sweet enough?" he growled sarcastically.

"No. That's not—"

"Any price you want, and it's yours, but in addition to Rawlins, I want you to leave Jackson and never see or talk to him again."

"I can't do that. I love him." She wiped away tears that were falling freely now.

"Pretty good act, but you don't love him. He's just a piece in the plan to get what you want."

Alex shook her head slowly, unable to fight the lies, unable to speak. Footsteps outside the door drew both their attention and when she heard the key sliding into the lock, she turned and ran to the bathroom before Jackson entered and found her crying.

"Well, howdy, youngster."

She pressed against the door and heard Everett's greeting. Jackson answered. His gruff voice was as sweet as music to her ears and she recognized the sound of pleasant surprise as he returned the greeting and asked where she was. Holding her breath, she waited for the older man to tell what he believed to be the truth, but he didn't, and suddenly she knew his plan. Jackson would never know. Everett wanted her to disappear without Jackson finding out what part he played.

If she told Jackson the truth, he was sure to take sides with the man who had mentored him, the man he loved as a father. She would lose him either way. Perhaps it was best to acquiesce to Everett's wishes. Perhaps it was foolish to think it would ever work, that it was ever meant to be.

"Hey, in there." Jackson rapped lightly at the bathroom door. "How beautiful do you have to be to get on a horse?"

She quickly wiped away the remaining tears. "I'll be there in just a minute." She ran cold water on the washrag and covered her eyes, hoping to erase the redness. Holding the cold cloth, she heard the rumbling of their voices in the next room. She would figure out a way. Alexandria Payne was not a loser. Alexandria Payne would find a way to keep the only man she ever truly loved if it took everything she had.

Minutes later, she emerged. "Ready?" She looked directly to Everett, daring him to do or say anything.

"You betcha," the older man said, gathering his hat from the dresser. "I'll meet you there later. I have to do a little more visiting."

His sly smile left no doubt in Alexandria's mind that he was not through with her.

"Done deal," Jackson said as he opened the door and waited for her.

Mechanically, Alexandria warmed up horses for Jackson. Her mind was definitely not focused on riding, but what Jackson taught her blended well with her natural ability. Trisha was there and rode circles around Jackson until he was forced to acknowledge her efforts. The two walked ahead of her, and Alex felt the pangs of not only jealousy, but of impending loss. If she were not there for Jackson, would he yield to Trisha's unceasing attack? Trisha's life certainly was more centered around his beloved cutting horses than hers had ever been, and, as difficult as it was to admit, Trisha was pretty, almost stunningly so. Would Jackson be happier with someone like her?

No. Trisha was toxic. She was spoiled and determined to have things Trisha's way. She was...everything Everett accused her of being. Logic told her they were a pair, but her heart told her there was a difference. She had changed. She loved Jackson. If it meant he would be happy, she would walk away from him in a minute. If only she knew what was best for him.

It was impossible not to watch him walk leisurely around the warm-up arena, speaking with people as he went, greeted by all, respected by all even though his name had been dragged through the dirt. She felt like an intruder, like a voyeur, watching from afar, lusting after the goodness that was Jackson Morgan. During his first two classes, Alex never felt more like an outsider. Jackson placed first in the Open Futurity class and second in the Open Derby class; each time he came first to her to share his success, but was quickly drawn away by others who wished him well.

Slowly the realization developed that, like the underdog, everyone wished him well. He'd been wronged and the cutting community, his family, rallied behind him when he accepted the punishment without comment. He was a gentleman to the end, and in the end, it brought him honor and respect that transcended whatever the world tried to do to tarnish it. Thinking about his personal fortitude, watching him ride like a human god, for the first time Alexandria began to really understand what had been missing from her life. Jackson was part of it, but the largest portion lay hidden within her.

Trotting toward her, his smile was infectious, demanding return. "Do me a favor and go to the trailer and get the bridle with the sweet iron bit."

"What's up? You don't usually forget anything."

"I know, I know," he said softly. "Please. I need it for the next class, and I'm deep in it with a woman who has three nice horses she'd like me to work with." A gleam entered his eye as he continued, "I'll make it worth your while..."

"I bet," Alex joked, her heart beating a little stronger just thinking about the offer. She reined toward the gate and eased her mare out and through the barn area to the trailer. Dismounting, she unlocked the tack room door and reached inside for the bridle. As she locked the door and turned back to the mare, she heard a voice from the side.

"I'm glad I found you alone."

Alex stopped, thought out carefully what she was going to say, then spun slowly on her heel to face the man connected to the voice.

"That's pretty much the way I feel, Paul."

"Trouble in paradise? My sympathies. Anything I can do?"

Alex laughed. "Oh, I think you've done enough. Why didn't you tell me you bought the loan on Jackson's ranch?"

"A quite brilliant move, if I do say so myself. It never hurts to hedge a bet."

She stared at the man she thought she knew. "At one time, I really thought you were special. How unfortunate for me that I seem to be in the middle of something you've created and for which *I'm* going to have to pay."

"You made the choice, Alexandria, darling. It's you who has changed. I sensed from the beginning of this deal that you were failing me. We have been such a good team for so long and it's due to the fact that we are the same person. You won't be happy with that cowboy. He can't possibly keep you interested once the rutting season is over."

Instantly, without the slightest warning, she slapped Paul. "You're disgusting."

He stood fast, still smiling. "I suppose I should be insulted, but your coarse boyfriend only proves your tastes have changed."

"There's more to him than you could ever hope to be."

"Well, again, I'm hurt. However, getting back to the reason for my visit. I see no reason to destroy our lucrative business arrangement just because we no longer are engaged. I am hoping you will come to your senses and pull through our difficulties."

Alex was stunned. She'd been so misled by their relationship, but perhaps he was right. If she did choose to leave Jackson, she'd have nowhere to go if not back to the life she'd known. Of course, there would be changes, but what else was left? The moment seemed to be rushing her toward a decision Alex was having a tough time making. Alexandria would have had no problem deciding. Could she set Alex aside and regain that barracuda attitude?

"Did you know about the connection between Covington and Jackson before I came here?"

"Of course. I thought you knew too, until you called excited by your finding. At that point, I thought it better not to tell you; after all, it was my way of letting you have the glory, so to speak."

She turned to the mare and prepared to mount up. "How kind." His hand gentle on her shoulder caused her to pause.

"I'm not heartless or without conscience, Alexandria. I just feel the need to fight for what's mine the only way I know how."

He pulled her to face him, but she looked at the reins in her hand. "You'll never know how much I want you back." He leaned forward and kissed her gently on the forehead. "I'll take you under any circumstances. I'm a proud man, but I'd even beg to have you back."

Alexandria was sick to her stomach. She turned and mounted, riding away without a word.

Alex felt like a thief, stealing happiness from the night. In her mind, Jackson had made sweet, gentle love to her with every word he had spoken. She tried not to think of it as the last time, but every time he whispered her name, she heard good-bye. By morning, she had made the decision to try her best to win. At the least, she would prove herself an apt student and Jackson a talented teacher. If he could say nothing else after she was gone, he could say she had learned well.

The next day Alex and Jackson prepared for their big ride. As they saddled, he made jokes about her not beating him too badly, but she knew he was trying to put her at ease and settle the nerves that had crept upon her like fog settles over the city. Both were riding novice horses and both used their warm-up time judiciously. Both were ringside when her name was called.

She looked at Jackson, who nodded and smiled encouragement. Her hand was trembling as she picked up the rein and urged the horse toward the herd. The palomino sensed tension and broke into a slow jog, but Alexandria quietly pulled him back to a walk and approached the herd.

Deciding on a black baldy cow that was fairly deep in the herd, Alex eased the gelding in, focusing on the particular animal she wanted. The palomino had his head down and hunted the cow perfectly. One by one, the surrounding cows peeled away, leaving the one in question. The yellow horse obeyed when Alex turned him loose and began working the cow. It felt good. Turn for turn, stop for stop, the gelding shadowed the animal who searched for a way back to the herd. Alex sat quietly, allowing the horse to show his stuff, falling into the rhythm. She was so glad to have picked a cow that showed the palomino's ability and that all was going well that she forgot time.

On the sideline, Jackson grew anxious as Everett rode up beside him.

"She needs to get off that one and get another," he said, prompted by nerves.

"I wouldn't worry about her, son. She'll come out all right."

"I want this for her more than I've ever wanted anything else in my life," Jackson said under his breath to no one but himself. He concentrated on her, willing her to hear him, and when she pulled up, perfectly timed, he was able to breathe again.

Alex collected herself for another try. The cow she chose this time left the herd easily, but stalled. Like water filling a glass, panic rose as Alex urged the gelding closer to get action from the cow. One good turn was all she got, and quickly she chose to quit the cow and get another. She realized time must be running out and tried to hurry, but just as she cut the third cow from the herd, the buzzer sounded.

Relieved that she'd ridden without any major errors, she patted the palomino's sleek neck as she exited and rode to Jackson. Before she got there, she saw Everett by his side, and once again the dead feeling gripped her chest and cut her breath in half.

"Good job," Jackson said, his gravelly voice sounding like heaven and hell all at once.

"Seventy-four," the announcer said in the background.

"I told you she was an expert," Everett said flatly, leaving her to wonder if he'd told Jackson anything. One look at the younger man confirmed he knew nothing.

"Go cool him out. You have enough time before my class starts," Jackson said, reaching out for her hand and tugging gently to bring her close enough for a quick kiss. He was vital and good. Alex suddenly felt guilty because *she* knew it couldn't last. Their hands lingered, touching as long as they could as she rode toward the warm-up pen to cool her horse off. Tearing herself away felt like a prelude to what was to come.

Several minutes later, crisp and fresh in a starched white shirt and jeans, Jackson rode into the arena as she rode up beside

Everett. If he loved Jackson, then surely he couldn't destroy him. He'd not hold her to the bargain that would kill them both, even though she'd never really agreed.

Jackson was totally focused on his horse and his job.

Sitting proudly astride his horse, Everett didn't look at her or acknowledge her presence. He was intent upon the man who began his first work in the arena. Alex focused on Jackson, not knowing or caring what score she'd received. He was poetry in motion as he became one with the sorrel horse. The mare herself wasn't flashy or attractive until he put her on a cow. Then she blossomed and grew beautiful under his guidance. Alex likened herself to the mare, reasoning that she had been only a fraction of what she could be until she met and trained with Jackson Morgan. He brought out the best in her as he did with the plain mare.

The first cow challenged the mare only slightly, and Alex knew she had much more to give. As if in agreement, Jackson quit and found another cow. It was a black one that looked a little wild, but Jackson must have been able to read it better than she, proving there was still more for her to learn. It began slowly hunting for a way back to the herd; then, after finding the sorrel blocking its escape each time, the animal picked up the pace. Jackson and the catty mare were there at every turn. Spectators whistled and hooted at turn after turn, and the more frustrated the cow became, the faster and better the mare worked.

Alex knew time was running out, that there was no way she could beat him. There was no animosity when she admitted defeat, only pleasure and admiration for the man she loved so dearly.

Suddenly, without any warning, Jackson pulled up.

The crowd moaned.

The buzzer sounded. He'd scored a hot quit after an unbelievable ride, and there wasn't a person horseback or afoot who didn't know he knew better and could have avoided it.

Alex was horrified. Like a shot to the gut, she realized what was going on. She looked to Everett, who was shocked but whose expression was stoic.

Head high, Jackson collected the mare and rode from the arena toward the trailer. Alex started to follow him, but Everett cut her off.

"You won, missy. Now go tell him good-bye."

"How can you do this? I won't do it, I can't do it."

Everett's face remained devoid of feeling. "He knows. I told him. You haven't got a snowball's chance in hell now."

Again, as if she'd just received a second Golden Gloves punch to the stomach, Alex wanted to double over and cry. The decision had been torn from her. She couldn't breathe, but it didn't matter; nothing mattered but Jackson.

"Go tell him good-bye. You owe him that much. Make a clean break."

She rode to the trailer, dismounting before she got there so she could watch him as he unsaddled. Slowly, painfully, she inched her way toward him. When she was within reach of the truck, she stopped.

"Jackson."

He halted with his back to her, but said nothing.

"You have to let me explain."

He spun, pain and anguish distorting his handsome face. "Explain. Yes," he growled fiercely, "explain to me why your ex-fiancé is here and was kissing you this morning. Explain it to me so I can understand how I poured my heart out to you last night and you forgot to tell me that he was back."

She'd never seen him so angry or so fearful, and his torture ripped through her heart like no other thing in the world could.

"While you're at it, explain how it slipped your mind that you were here only so you could cheat Everett and lie to me." He stepped forward and stood inches from her, his animal instincts wild and savage as he glared into her. "I beg your pardon, lying would have been too direct. You just never mentioned it at all."

As a sail loses wind, so his arms drooped to his sides and there was a look of defeat and betrayal to him that made her want to look away. Steeling herself to her own pain, she waited until he had nothing more to say.

"Jackson. I've made some mistakes, but—"

"But what?" he began again. "Are you going to tell me you love me? I guess I was warned right from the beginning, but I went ahead not once, but twice. I even told you I was being honest and you agreed it was the right thing for us…to start over, you said."

"I do love you."

"That's scary, Alex—no, Alexandria. I don't think I can afford your love. It may cost me my ranch. Or is your boyfriend going to let me keep that? My last fiasco with a woman left me with my dignity, but this one…" His face contorted in disgust.

"Please." Tears began to fall. "Please let me talk."

He straightened up and ripped the rein from her hand. "Go ahead. But stop crying. It's so unlike you."

She drew several deep breaths to stop the flow of tears, aware he watched every movement. "I admit when I first came here, I did have a purpose. But I never told you otherwise. It wasn't part of our bargain, just like it wasn't part of our bargain for me to fall in love with you." She turned and began to pace in front of him, like a caged animal. "It came so quickly. One minute we were sparring over where I was going to sleep and the next I was wishing you were there with me." She hesitated, searching his face for some trace of understanding, a glimmer of hope. "I started by keeping my business, including Paul, separate from what was happening with you." She touched his sleeve and he pulled away. "Then it was suddenly too late for a confession. I realize now what a mistake it was, but beyond that, and more important, I realize what I've thrown away."

“The way Everett tells it, you’ve won. You have everything you wanted.”

She stood before him, blue eyes pleading her case. “No. I’ve lost everything. You are the sunshine in my life. Your laugh is food for my soul, and my heart is yours.”

“Isn’t that a song? Isn’t there anything about you that’s genuine?”

Time stood still as Alexandria clung to reality by a thread. A lifetime of wheeling and dealing left her totally unprepared for this.

He cleared his throat and tried to speak after a long silence between them when all else seemed superfluous. It came as a whisper, and before he spoke, she thought there might be hope.

“Good-bye, Alexandria.”

CHAPTER 9

Alex watched him put away his saddle and walk around the corner of the barn. When he disappeared, something inside her died. There was an emptiness, a hole in her heart and soul that seemed to have no end. She stood silent, dead to the world. Time had no relevance, and if lightning had struck next to her, Alex wouldn't have known because his good-bye felt like a slab of concrete falling on her.

In her whole life she'd never felt so worthless. When her mother died, there'd been anger and loneliness, but she'd survived. As a young girl, she had even survived her father's continued absence. Then later, he made it clear that she wasn't worth his time unless she could steamroll Wall Street the way he'd done. Alexandria hadn't let it be an obstacle for too long. A slow, smoldering anger at being kept from those she loved most burned inside her until she had developed Alexandria Payne—corporate raider, financial wonder who needed no one. Once the fire began, it was insatiable, and the crowning victory had been when her father had come to her, begging for money to save his crumbling empire.

She'd given it freely, without any emotional strings, but only because it had been a profitable arrangement. Alexandria Payne was at the top of the dog-eat-dog business world, but, after a month of living in dirt, dust, and manure with a simple cowboy, she had slowly come to the realization that she couldn't have gotten any lower when it came to being human. The lowest she'd ever been was the moment, only seconds ago, that she discovered that Jackson's good-bye meant more to her than all the money on Wall Street.

"Alexandria?"

Like a distant echo from behind her, she heard her name. Unless it was Jackson who called, she had no wish to answer, but she heard it again.

"My God. What has that brute done to you?"

Like a vague sixth sense, she understood that Paul's arm circled her shoulder and drew her close, but there was nothing lifelike or warm about it. She felt nothing as he ushered her toward the parking lot, chattering the whole time.

"Say something, Alexandria. Tell me what a fool I am for letting you out of my sight, tell me what a cad he is." He stopped and took her by the shoulders and shook her. "Say something."

She forced herself to focus on the perfect, patrician face before her. "I'm so tired. I need to sit."

"Of course," Paul said as he unlocked the door to his rented Mercedes and opened it, gesturing to the fine leather seat. "Here. I have Perrier in the back; I'll get it. Stay here."

She heard someone laugh halfheartedly and was barely able to believe it had been her. As if she had anywhere to go. Disgusted and hating herself for failing to close the biggest deal of her life, she slumped in the seat.

Paul returned, dropping to his knees as he handed her the bottle. "Sorry I don't have a straw, but drink it anyway. I'll look the other way if you like."

He was genuinely concerned, she thought. She found no joy in that fact, thinking only that she didn't want or need the straw, the water, or Paul. She drank anyway and began to look around her. Horse trailers, pickup trucks, manure carts—the distant sound of the announcer, nearby horses stomping in their stalls, and the satisfying smell of alfalfa hay and pine shavings. These were things that had become a part of her life with Jackson, and these were things unavailable to her without him. It was no use. She didn't belong here anymore.

"Please take me home."

Paul jumped to her request as if he'd been shot. "Oh yes. You can tell me what happened on the way," he said as he ran to the driver's side and jumped in. The glaring look she sent set him back momentarily. "Or you can keep the sordid story to yourself, my dear."

"You didn't close my door," she said, struggling to save what was left of her pride, ordering herself to be Alexandria who demanded more than most were willing to give—not Alex who enjoyed a simple sunset, who liked the taste of powdered lemonade, and who loved Jackson with every ounce of her being. Paul jumped again, shut her door, and returned to his seat while she primped, smoothing her disheveled hair as she looked in the visor mirror, just as she would have done a month ago. "I'll send for my things."

Paul smiled and nodded. "I'll have you home in an hour, and I'll call ahead and instruct Hesperia to—"

"I just want to be alone."

Alexandria knew how flat and expressionless her voice was, but didn't know how to change it. At this point, her world *was* flat and expressionless. She needed to figure out where to go from here.

An hour later, Paul's Mercedes slowed and stopped at the palatial brass and copper entry of her luxury apartment. She instructed him to drop her at the door, then leave her alone. At the entrance the doorman stopped her.

"Are you…visiting…someone here?"

She looked up, straightened herself, and tossed an appropriately insulted look his way.

"Miss Payne," he said quickly as he offered to help her with the huge door. "I'm so sorry. You're not dressed, that is, I've never seen you—"

"Don't worry, Howard." She strutted inside. "I realize I look a sight. You'll have to let me in since I don't have my purse."

"Right away, madam." He dug in his pocket. "In fact, you take the key and I can get it when you come down next."

She took it, went to the elevator, and within minutes she was inside what used to be home. She closed the door and lay back against it, casually observing the pristine white living room that spread before her to the left. It was beautiful, in an *Architectural Digest* kind of way, but it wasn't warm and inviting like that modest mobile home had been. She tossed the key on the entry table, but the feeling that she didn't belong here kept her back. Somewhere beyond the black-out shades that stretched across the broad living room wall, the sun was setting. Somewhere outside the triple-pane windows, birds sang and creeks gurgled. Jackson lived in a place where birds sang for him and where the sun warmed him. She missed him already.

Salty tears blurred Alexandria's vision and dribbled down the mahogany door to the floor, splashing on the polished parquet like raindrops forgotten on the barren desert. She lay down, lacking the will or the energy to remain upright, wishing there was a way to either end it all or to begin all over again.

For hours she lay on the cold, hard wood, remembering fleeting moments of happiness that seemed like jewels stolen from a treasure chest. The way his lips felt upon hers. His smile when he was proud of her. The instant she first saw him. Even then, she'd been struck by his power, by his gentleness, by his love of life.

Small bits and pieces were all she knew about him, all he'd given to her, and wouldn't have been enough to fall in love with another man, but this man had fit her like a single seed fits in the smallest fissure of a giant rock, then grows to be a tree, bold and upright. His quiet strength, his soft growl, his dry humor were all a part of the magic that entwined her to him just like the honeysuckle by the creek tangled around the grandfather oak and softened its rigid lines. He was the oak and she the tangled vine. She rolled to her back, wiped at her tears, and closed her eyes to draw upon more images of them together. It eased the pain to remember.

Only now did she understand how happy she'd been then, and perhaps that was what was going to save her. The fact that she'd found happiness and contentment, be it only one second out of a whole lifetime, was miraculous, something many people never experienced. Maybe she'd been so greedy for the largest part of her life that this was her punishment. *To want more desperately, urgently—and to be denied. The ultimate denial. Prohibition of the heart and soul. The knowledge that it was and now* is *no longer.*

A week had gone by since Alexandria had come face-to-face with the reality that she'd lost Jackson. Like an artist who swabs paint over a mistake, she let the trappings of her former life encase her feelings. As far as anyone knew, she'd returned as planned, triumphant as usual, but the wound to her soul festered beneath and was clearly visible in her eyes had anyone taken the time to see it.

Paul had been every inch a gentleman, having never mentioned Jackson, Covington, or even COMJET. There were brief moments that hit like déjà vu when Alexandria teetered on the edge of reality, wondering if that month had been a beautiful dream. Then the memory of Jackson's fiery embrace burned through any notion that he was only a dream. Once Jackson entered her mind, the only thing that could drive him out was forced hours of strict attention to detail, hours of dealing with figures, people, and new plans of attack.

Her desk was cluttered with proposals, messages to be returned, and synopses of failed or faltering businesses. Alexandria was intent upon a central stack of papers whose figures she read off to the anonymous person on the other end of the phone conversation.

"No. You don't have that kind of clout with the bank balance that I see here." She leaned back, flipped the financial statement shut, and tossed her pen on top. "Why don't you take a second look at what you've sent me and then call me back. I think I can help, but not without a little more…honesty on your part. We have to be talking apples to apples here." There was a moment of silence, then she replied as there was a gentle knock on her door. "Fine. I'll expect to hear from you early next week."

"Yes?" she said as she hung up and began writing.

"This just came by messenger," Paul said as he walked in, Armani clad and as smug as if he held the winning Lotto ticket. He sat smiling on the corner of her desk.

"Don't play games," she said, still looking down. "What is it?"

Paul tapped the large manila envelope in his lap, but said nothing. Finally he tossed it on her desk.

"What—" She stopped as soon as she saw the return address. Her eyes flitted to him and then back to the envelope. She reached for it. "You opened it."

"Yes. I didn't think you'd mind. After all, we're—"

"Of course," she interrupted, her breath already sticking in her throat and her heart beginning to beat faster. "What does Everett—Covington want?"

"It's the contract for Rawlins. Signed, sealed, and ready to record."

She stood up, crossed her arms, and walked to the huge window that overlooked the smoggy Los Angeles skyline. "Send it back."

"What!"

She spun and faced him, like a tigress on the prowl. "You heard me, send it back. I don't want anything to do with it."

"COMJET won't go without it, especially at this late date."

"Then it won't go. I don't want anything to do with Rawlins or Covington and that's final."

Paul stood and faced her as he ran his hands in the pockets of his tailored pants. He rocked back and forth gently, and by the twisted look of his handsome face, it was obvious he was scheming. "Final." He paced in front of her, for effect, not from nervousness. "We have spent thousands of dollars, and now you have victory within your grasp and you won't take it."

A flood of emotions crept through Alexandria's mind, and instead of answering his challenge with a bold, sweeping statement, all she could manage was weak and soft. "That's right. I know you think I've lost my competitive edge, but I need you to understand why I can't do it."

His pacing began to be more determined, more furious as he spoke. He fixed his glare on the floor ahead of him and spoke through gritted teeth. "I understand more than you think. You have run off looking for God knows what in the arms of a ragamuffin country lout. You had nothing in common with him and there was no way in the world it ever could have worked out."

"That's not so," she rebutted without conviction.

"Get real, Alexandria. You are a Vassar graduate, you have countless business awards and degrees, like it or not, you were raised with a silver spoon in each hand, and you think you could have taken a common laborer in and made it work?"

He stopped. His glare was punishing. "Admit it, you've been a fool who thought a weekend lark, a summer romance"—he waved his arms while his cold blue eyes narrowed to their target—"an overnight stand, if you will, was going to last. The truth is, you've fallen for this cowboy and now he's thrown you out." Silence punctuated his words.

"You owe him nothing. You owe me a lot." He leaned across her desk toward her. "Alexandria, pay up."

Jackson had struggled just to make it through the rest of the classes at Temecula. Everett was by his side and prodded and cajoled, but Jackson was cold and silent. He'd trusted the woman with his heart, and she'd used and betrayed him without a second thought.

The long drive home had been tedious and exhausting, and he was acutely aware that she was no longer sitting next to him, no longer laughing with him, no longer smiling that sly, crooked little grin when she knew he was right, no longer pretending to be his.

Tired, worn, and disgusted with life, Jackson dragged himself from the barn after he'd put up all the horses, unloaded the trailer, and cleaned the tack. It was late; a sliver of moon produced only enough light to cast an eerie gleam on the mobile home that was dark and lifeless. He knew he'd stalled as long as possible. The wooden porch creaked as he stepped up. He hesitated before he opened the screen, then opened the door and tossed his duffel bag on the floor and stopped.

As soon as he drew a breath, he smelled her, and for an instant, he wondered if she was in the bedroom. Then reality hit. Will—like a fairy tale white knight—had banished her from his kingdom, chased the evil witch away, and now he was alone with only his honor, his good name, and his thoughts to keep him company. He'd been a chivalrous fool to think the slick, high-maintenance city woman really cared. But of course he was wiser now, and like Merlin, he wanted to make every trace of her disappear.

He strolled through the darkness to the kitchen bar. The jealous green eye of the answering machine blinked over and over. For a moment he hoped it was her, pleading with him to take her back and admitting how devious she'd been, but as he slowly reached for the button, he thought twice. A lot of good it did to erase her from his mind when he allowed her to return so easily. He drew his hand back and turned to the refrigerator. The light blinded him briefly as he opened the door, but he thrust his hand inside, knowing exactly where the lemonade was.

He took a long drink from the pitcher because he knew she would have made him use a glass. He gulped, the cold tart taste soothing the burn in his gut. Bringing the pitcher down as the refrigerator door slid shut, he saw again the green reflection from the answering machine. He'd never run from a thing in his life, and he wasn't going to start now. He set the pitcher down as if to mark his spot and very deliberately punched the button.

As soon as he recognized the pleasant tones of Everett's slow drawl, Jackson exhaled. He had urgent business, but he would come by as soon as he was finished.

It was almost a relief to hear Everett—almost. His mind wandered as he put the lemonade away. What would he do if she did apologize and beg his forgiveness? He had never believed in forgiveness, only hard work and honesty. If a person worked hard at being honest, there was never a need to be forgiven. Or did he need to reassess the reasons he was who he was?

He drew a deep breath and admitted that his mind was going in circles. He needed to be practical. It was a moot point anyway. She would never say she was sorry and be sincere, much less beg him to take her back, but that was fine. He rotated his head to ease the tension in his neck and shoulders. He was tired. The drive had taken everything out of him, and Jackson knew he should get some sleep.

Out of habit he stumbled toward his office and the lumpy couch. One look at it and he turned to *his* bedroom. He walked down the hall to his room as if he were sneaking up on a burglar, and when he pushed the door open, he felt like an intruder in his own home. Flipping the light on, he gazed across the dresser, filled with her cosmetic army of expensive bottles and tubes. Her clothes were in his closet, and her hairbrush was on his nightstand. Immediately the urge to bag everything that was hers and throw it out struck and he swept everything from the dresser.

Get a grip, Morgan. He wasn't normally an impulsive person, given to rash decisions. *If she wants them, let her send someone to get them. Unlikely. She'd just buy more.* He pulled the tail of his shirt from his pants and slowly, methodically unbuttoned the front before he stripped it off. Next he slowly unbuckled his silver buckle and pulled the belt from the loops, then kicked off his boots and fell back on the bed.

By morning, he'd risen twice for more lemonade, changed the bed sheets because he couldn't stand the overpowering aroma of honeysuckle, found out the smell was coming from a bottle that had broken when he'd cleared the dresser, and sat for forty-five minutes on the back lawn, looking at the stars before he finally gave up and went out to feed just before dawn broke.

Like a machine, he moved from one task to another, not allowing himself time to rest because there was so much to do after being gone for a long weekend and because he knew thoughts of her would creep like a plague back into his mind if he didn't keep busy.

He rode horses despite the heat, pushing each one to the limit, and then saddling another, driving himself to the brink of exhaustion. He never admitted that Alexandria was his taskmaster, his private demon.

It was early evening the next day when Everett drove in to find Jackson splitting wood.

"Jehoshaphat, son," he said as he stretched out of the shiny diesel dually. "Didn't I teach you to come in outta the rain and stay in the shade when it's over a hundred?"

Jackson wiped his brow. The sweat poured from his temples and ran down his naked back and shoulders. "You taught me that if I don't chop wood, then I'm gonna be cold as hell all winter."

"Well, it's gonna be winter before you cool down. Take pity on an old man and let's go inside and get us something to drink."

Jackson shook his head and set the ax down. "You go. I have to finish."

Everett pursed his lips and then answered. "I can probably still whip you if I need to, son. Why don't you make it easy on us both and come on in."

Jackson eyed him cautiously before he turned and headed for the house.

"I'll have a beer," Everett said when they arrived. "You got anything to eat?"

Jackson drank greedily, the cold water tasting better than he'd expected. "Nope. Guess you'll have to go into town."

"Good idea. We'll take a break and eat at the Sloughhouse Inn, my treat."

"Nope." Jackson slammed the glass on the counter. "You go. Bring me a doggie bag."

"Tarnation but you're obnoxious today."

Jackson looked at the older man. "Sorry. I don't mean to be, but I'm not good company anymore. I—"

"Cowboy up, fella." He came to Jackson's side and put a loving arm around his shoulders. "You been stomped on twice now by women, and I know this last one was gettin' to you, but I know you got it in you to see that life goes on and you've got a lot to look forward to."

Jackson pulled away to refill his glass. "You're right. I know it. And I'm not down by a long shot. I just need a little time to myself to think." He leaned on the kitchen counter and held his glass high. "To finding two women who will clean stalls, ride a horse, and…." A quiet but solemn smile spread across his face. "And love the hell outta us."

Everett laughed with him. "And not take us to the poorhouse in the meantime."

Jackson forced himself to perk up for Everett's sake, and for the remainder of the two days Everett stayed, he was as cordial as he knew how. There were times when it felt like the old days, but many more when he knew deep inside that Alexandria had changed him forever. The trick now was to outlive the problems she'd caused him.

When Everett said good-bye, his last words repeated in Jackson's mind later that evening. "Don't let her make you bitter, son. There's a lot of sunshine that's free for the taking."

Easier said than done, he thought as he boiled spaghetti. She'd betrayed them both and the fact that she had broken through the layers of protection he'd laid so carefully continued to eat away at his sense of well-being. It seemed that now simple survival was the only thing left. He drained and buttered his pasta. *Not gourmet, but filling*, he thought.

He sat, alone, eating spaghetti with no sauce, searching his soul for answers. All his life, he'd put honesty on a pedestal: if he was angry with her for not being honest, then he had to be honest with himself and admit that the part that made him most bitter was the fact that from the moment he first saw her, he'd been drawn to her like a bee to honey. Something about her had blinded him and made him think he had a chance when she had told him right away that he had none.

She'd made him believe, she'd made him laugh, and like a classic tale, she'd led him to a tragedy. She'd made him love her. Just like the song—"Fools rush in where wise men never go. Wise men never fall in love."

CHAPTER 10

Less than a week after Temecula her check arrived by messenger. Just like lightning striking too near, seeing her precise handwriting on the envelope made Jackson tense. He tossed it on the kitchen counter and tried to ignore it while he fixed lunch, but it called to him like a Siren calls to a sailor. Finally he opened it. There was no greeting, no note, only the check for ten thousand plus three thousand "for expenses" as it said on the check.

It was hard to ride Hattie. Jackson seemed to have lost the knack of dealing with the mare who, if he hadn't known better, seemed to be pining away for Alex. Before, the horse had been docile and willing, but now she put her ears back when he came with a halter and then sulled up when he rode her. It took all the patience and know-how he possessed to get through a twenty-minute workout. It seemed that Hattie had picked up her stubborn, obstinate attitude from Alexandria.

The days were beginning to reflect the slow approach of fall. Daylight hours were shrinking and the evenings growing. Jackson had no shortage of horses to ride and even had a waiting list of clients eager to bring babies to him for training. The two-year financial drought brought on by the fines, and the suspension, and by trusting the wrong people were over, but the barren desert of his soul had just begun its odyssey.

Every evening he found himself wandering out to see Joker. He grabbed a couple of brushes and went to Joker's pasture where he brushed the aging black body until it was glossy and shiny. He ran his hand over Joker's neck and played with his mane. The horse was a loyal trouper; he was the childhood friend who never thought poorly of the boy who had nothing going for him and who always had the patience to forgive him while he was learning.

Jackson lost himself for a moment in memories of his first cutting victories—victories made possible by the old horse, victories that tasted like honey to a child who had none. Joker nudged him, his soft muzzle prodding, searching for more attention.

"Not enough ear rubbing for you, huh, fella." He massaged the knot on top of the horse's head and ran his fingers around the swelling at the base of each ear while Joker leaned into him, begging for more. "If I could take twenty years off your life, we'd be a team again." He hugged the horse's neck. "We're still a team—you and me. We still need each other."

It was hard to think about need without Alex creeping into the picture, but Jackson kept telling himself that obsession and dependency were unhealthy, that she was only a passing fancy. He stroked Joker's silken forehead and remembered how the horse had taken to her. "I suppose if I asked you about her, you'd tell me the truth."

The old horse snorted, a sneeze of sorts.

"Of course you would," he said, sadness filling in the silence as he patted the gelding. "I won't be here for a couple days. Juan will, though. This is a biggie for me, the first National show since, well, since the trouble." The old gelding's ears perked and he seemed to be listening. "I wish you could be there with me for moral support." Joker rubbed on Jackson's chest as if moral support could be had by osmosis. "Anyway, hang in there. I'll be back."

Life had been simple for the last month since she'd left, and although it hurt to say her name, the thought of her brought sadness instead of searing pain. Jackson had gone on living, working with breakneck intensity, climbing to the top of his profession without missing a step.

He planned to take six horses to Ogden, Utah, to the National Cutting Horse Association Western Nationals. Money had been added to every purse, and if the extraordinarily rich pots weren't enough, it was a Championship Cutting, which meant that placing counted as points toward the cutting horse of the year award. Everyone who was anyone on the West Coast would be there. Everett was coming, and Jackson knew he'd see many old friends. Normally, it would be something he looked forward to with a child's eagerness, but right now, as he packed, he couldn't say there was any overwhelming joy in his heart.

Everett was the one exception. Jackson welcomed the sight of the Texan who was more than a father to him. It was a matter of things infinitely more important than blood. Everett had always been there when he needed him and never had condemned him for doing things his own way. He owed the man his life; had he not met him, he would probably have gone the way of countless other juvenile delinquents. Jackson would always have a special place in his heart for the man and that was what made it so difficult to forgive or forget Alexandria's plan to manipulate him. As he hooked the truck to the trailer, he couldn't understand why there was any question in his mind where his allegiance lay.

Two days later, with four of his horses and two of Everett's that had been with him for a month or so, he pulled into Ogden's Golden Spike arena. He was exhausted, partially by the drive, but partially from hours alone, trying to settle the turbulent waters of his mind. He drove to the stables and unloaded the horses. He was feeding the last one when he heard Trisha's always-on voice behind him as he turned.

"Jackson, darling." She marched up, trapped his head between her hands, and kissed him on the mouth. "Where have you been hiding? I've been telling everyone I see what a fantastic trainer you are, but really, I didn't intend for you to be working all the time." Her hands dribbled down his cheeks, over his neck, and rested possessively on his chest.

He leaned over, set the feed bucket down, then straightened and calmly removed her hands and set them by her sides. "Hello, Trisha. You're right. I've been busy, and thank you for sending the Praters to me. They have several really well-bred two-year-olds that I am going to like working with."

He stooped for the bucket and began walking toward the truck.

Trisha followed. "Don't I get a reward for finding them?"

He stopped and turned to find she had also stopped and now stood with an incredibly pouty expression that demanded attention.

"Let satisfaction be your reward, Trisha." He walked on. "Are you showing that little bay horse you bought from Carol Rose?" Her exasperated sigh behind him was the first clue that she was losing patience.

She wiggled her way to him as he tucked the bucket in the bed of the pickup. "Let's start over, Jackson. I know that trashy woman from Los Angeles is gone, and I know that whatever she did to you—"

Jackson had a slow fuse, but Trisha was playing with dynamite and didn't know it. "Drop it, Trisha."

"No. I can see how much she's hurt you, and I want you to know I'm here if you want to talk." She pressed her tiny body along his backside and ran her hand along the length of his arm.

The feel of her made Jackson sick in the same way he'd feel if a snake had slithered over his body. He turned on her, swallowing his disgust, trying to be gentle as he set her away. "A lot has passed between us, Trisha." He hesitated. "But I don't think either one of us really wants to start over."

"You're wrong, Jackson. I do want to start over. I want you to treat me like you used to, not like everyone else. I want you to forgive—"

"I can't." He turned his back on her and pretended to search for something behind the truck seat.

Trisha grabbed his arm and pulled him around. "You mean you won't. I made one little mistake and you're never going to let me forget it—you're going to punish me forever."

He drew a deep breath and looked directly into her smoldering eyes. "It has nothing to do with punishment, and no, I probably won't forget that you nearly ruined my career as a cutter and you almost made me lose my ranch."

"I would have given you the money."

"That's the point, Trisha. Everett would have given me the money. It wasn't the money as much as it was all the rest."

"I tried to hire a lawyer for you."

"And I refused." He stepped toward her, his features growing harder even though his eyes were tired. "We've been through this a thousand times and it never gets any better."

"I know," she said, sticking her nose in the air and looking very defensive. "I should have sent the papers in on that mare, and yes, I knew when I entered that I was illegal. The drugs were a big mistake, but she was sore. And yes, I know now that when I was caught, I should have played ignorant or something that didn't involve arguing and going after that judge."

He shook his head. Hearing her recap brought it back all too clearly. The anger, the embarrassment, having his name published in dishonor, the court hearing. The resurgence of all the ugly rumors and the year of suspension when he wasn't allowed to show or earn money in the cutting horse industry were all because of the woman standing before him, who now wanted him to forget how it felt to have his good name and reputation dragged through the mud.

Jackson stood silent and strong. "If you aren't careful, you'll get caught again with your pants down, Trisha. There are a lot of people around to hear you."

She sniffed, probably for effect. "How can you still be mad for one mistake? I've told you how sorry I am that I involved you. Everybody knows you had nothing to do with it; it's just that you were a trainer and—"

"And I should have known better," he said, frustration boiling to the surface. "The bottom line is that I was the one who paid for it, and it's done. I have the money to pay off the balloon on my ranch, I'm back in good standing with the cutting horse association, and I have a full barn. Drop it, Trisha. Drop it right now, and don't expect me to be anything more than polite to you. You don't really want me anyway; you want another trophy, and so far you haven't got a Jackson Morgan in your collection. At one time, I thought you were a friend to me—"

"We were more than friends," she whispered, seeming hurt.

"Maybe, but you never treated me in a loving way. You never cared if I was happy, you never took the time to watch the sun set with me..." His voice slowed as he realized what he was saying. He swallowed hard. "You never insisted that I take a long look at life and see what good things I already had."

For several seconds there was nothing but silence between them.

Trisha put her hands on her hips. "I can do more for you than she can."

He continued to be silent.

"She's not even here."

Jackson's mind danced with a million scattered thoughts. He'd banished her, but he had no choice. She'd betrayed him. He hadn't listened when she tried to explain. She'd given up on them. She was the most beautiful thing in his life, yet she'd done the ugliest kind of thing to him. He turned, and for the first time, he knew why a swan grieved the loss of a mate. He knew why the lone wolf sat on a mountaintop and howled.

He took one last look at Trisha and felt nothing but pity. "I have survived everything you've done to me, but you are still fighting for something you can't quite put a name to. I'd like to say I will help you, but I have to go pick up Everett at the airport. Good luck tomorrow."

He got in his pickup and started the engine. Ten minutes later, he watched Everett land. An hour later they were in the Mexican restaurant at the crossroad, finishing dinner.

"I got a side bet with Lester Murray. He says I can't beat him on two out of three works—any ones I choose." Everett sipped ice tea between sentences, then set the glass down when he noticed Jackson's silence. "You want part of the action, son?"

Jackson shook his head. "No. Can't say I want any part of that deal." His mind flitted back to Everett's bet with Alexandria.

"Come on. Last time you won a dinner." Everett leaned back in his chair eyeing Jackson. "It's a friendly wager."

Jackson ran his fingers up and down the iced tea glass, making tracks in the condensation.

"Look." Everett leaned forward and set his elbows on the table. "I can see straight through you. You're still pining for that woman."

Never losing focus of the tracks in the glass, Jackson answered. "I can't get her out of my mind. Everywhere I go, she's there, and everything I do, I remember doing it with her or think about how she'd like it."

Everett was sure nothing he said would ease Jackson's mind. "I knew when you fell for something in tight Wranglers and a hair ribbon, you'd fall hard."

He looked to the older man. "Thanks for the confidence builder. I'm trying to forget her, not have you tell me how impossible it is."

"I don't mean to interfere, but—"

Suddenly Jackson spoke up. "Then speaking of bets, why did you bet Rawlins? Why did you set her up for the fall?"

"Now wait a minute. The pot is calling the kettle black. You were the one who threw away that last work so she could win, so she could take Rawlins."

"I had to know if she would do it, but I ask you again, why did *you* do it?"

"You know me, I can't resist gambling a little." Each word bounced carelessly across his lips, but then he stopped, regarding Jackson as a man with a serious problem—one that he had helped create, one that deserved an honest answer. His second try was more sober. "I checked up on her as soon as I met her because I didn't want you getting into another mess like the one with Trisha. She was offering you easy money and you were taking it faster than a deacon takin' up a collection."

"You shouldn't have interfered."

"Maybe so, but in defense of myself, as soon as I found out she was APM, the outfit that had tried to move heaven and earth to buy Rawlins, I figured she had something up her sleeve. I needed to find out as much as you needed to find out if she would take the bait."

Jackson's vacant gaze was still fixed on Everett, and he knew if he ever cared about the boy he'd helped raise, that he couldn't stop here. He took a long, deep drink of tea when Jackson said nothing and then it was his turn to play with the glass.

"She didn't."

"Didn't what?"

"She didn't take the bait."

Jackson rose a little and grabbed Everett's weathered hand. "Alex didn't buy Rawlins?"

"No." Everett watched interest rise in the young man's face.

"You mean you never agreed on terms?"

"No. I mean she turned it down flat. I sent her several contracts, the last one practically gave it to her for a nickel, but she sent them all back. When I tried to talk to her, she wouldn't answer my calls. Paul Maitland was pretty bent out of shape about it as I hear, but she refused."

Jackson sat back. "Then nobody got a damn thing out of this whole mess."

"You can change that."

"No, the damage has been done. I can't forget Trisha and I can't forget—"

Everett stood up, digging in his pocket. "I thought I taught you that 'I can't' doesn't belong in your vocabulary."

Jackson watched Everett throw money for the bill on the table, then turn and walk toward the door. Ever since he could remember, Everett had led him to water and then let him decide whether or not to drink. He could feel the cool taste of water on his lips, but wasn't sure he wanted to swallow.

Everett strolled to the truck and Jackson followed. The evening air still had a hint of heat left over from the day, but for the most part, it felt like the kind of evening that makes a person want to breathe deep and stretch. Jackson breathed deep all right, but he wasn't relaxed enough to stretch.

The rest of the night and most of the next morning, he and Everett avoided the topics of Rawlins, laying bets, and Alexandria, but she was as much in Jackson's mind as ever. He rode in three classes the next day, and for the next three days, each work came up with scores good enough to put him in the top five for the finals in two classes. Everett took him to dinner to celebrate, and between a few rounds of Jack Daniels and lots of horse, cutting, and people talk, it was late before they hit the sheets.

Jackson was tired and knew better than to stay up late before another full day of showing, but suspected he might sleep better if he was completely worn out.

He was wrong. About one thirty he was still awake and angry with himself for not sleeping. He'd tossed and turned, driven Alex from his mind several times and made mental plans for the way he was going to ride each horse to its fullest. Finally he turned on the television and settled back, hoping to be bored into sleep.

He found a local cable sports program and saw the last half of a Forty-Niners game. Afterwards, he was still quite awake and watched the news. Nothing new, the same crime and no punishment, followed by a sportscaster whose neck looked to be as big as Jackson's thigh. Suddenly the picture switched to a taped segment on the cutting horse show that was in town, and Jackson's interest rose slightly.

The newscaster interviewed several well-known trainers and competitors first, then took a tour of the stables, trying to show how laid back these expensive horses were. Then the camera switched to a sweeping view of the audience during the competition, and while the discussion moved to an interview with the show manager, Jackson saw her.

He sat upright in bed as if he'd been struck by a thunderbolt. The camera stayed in one place, but in the background he saw Alex at a vendor's booth. He was sure it was her. Her blonde hair was done in a braid he'd recognize anywhere, and when she turned toward the camera and walked away with her drink, her face was sober and serious.

Then she was gone.

The sports reporter's words were a garbled jumble and might as well have been Greek to Jackson. He didn't know what to do or think. Then he took a deep breath.

Logically, the only reason Alexandria would be here was to continue her mission to get to Everett. Throwing the Rawlins contract back in his face had probably been a strategic attempt at manipulation to get a better deal, and she was here to close it.

Strange. Everett hadn't mentioned seeing her or hearing from her. His throat was suddenly very dry, and he ripped the sheet from his body. He stomped to the bathroom to get a drink of water. Everett seemed to be softening about her. Maybe. Until she stepped back in for the kill. If that was so, that would explain his dropping the subject. It wasn't like him to quit on something he thought was right. But perhaps he also neglected to mention her in order to keep from twisting the knife Alex had left in his back.

He swallowed hard and set the glass down. He was rambling like the village idiot. The face before him in the mirror used to have lines created by laughter, but now there were equally deep lines in his forehead generated by a month of frustration.

He turned the light off and lumbered back to bed. Lying alone in the early morning glow of the television, he cursed the day he'd met her. His life hadn't been perfect before her, but at least he had peace of mind. At least he had control of a life he'd fought so hard to manage. Before Alexandria Payne, he'd had control.

It set her heart all aflutter just to see him. He was warming up a horse; it looked like the little sorrel mare that came in for training just before…before Temecula, before he'd thrown her out. He still rode like a king, proud and confident, and he still had an air about him that would have made him stand out from all the rest even if she didn't love him.

When a representative of APM had been asked to a meeting of the board of directors of a company based in Salt Lake, she'd been the one to go since Paul was busy with a buyer from England. At the time, she had no idea that a cutting extravaganza would be so close at the same time. She had seen it advertised the first day she had come and then argued with herself for two days before she finally went.

The first work she'd seen had been smooth and aggressive, just the way the judges like to see a horse, and Jackson had scored

151. Sitting in the stands, she was privy to scattered comments about the contestants and horses. It was his family, Alexandria remembered. People who looked to be real cutters usually had good things to say about Jackson. Occasionally there was a quick reference to the scandal, but it was clear that those who knew him thought he'd been unfairly judged. An older couple seated directly in front of her seemed to know the most, although they were closemouthed about the specifics.

When the performance was over, Alexandria wanted to confirm that Everett had given her the straight story.

"Pardon me, I'm considering Jackson Morgan as a trainer, and I couldn't help but overhear what you were saying." The white lies slipped out effortlessly. She knew Jackson wouldn't approve, but she needed to know the truth about his past and if he was in some bind that she had made worse. "Would you mind telling me more?"

The woman, wearing an expensive silver Concho necklace with amber stones, waved her hand, a prelude to setting Alexandria's mind at ease. "Of course not. Tell her, Bert." The man opened his mouth to speak, but she cut him off.

"It wasn't his fault, you know, and I would recommend the young man. Are you familiar with the National Cutting Horse Association?"

"A little," Alexandria said truthfully.

"Tell her about the rules, Bert."

Alexandria suspected the two were married, but when again Bert did little more than open his mouth before she interrupted, it seemed a certainty.

"There are a lot of rules about ownership, and a non-pro or an amateur rider must ride their own horse in most classes."

Bert nodded in the background. Alexandria smiled at both of them.

"Well, he had a client who had been taking lessons on a particular horse and wanted to buy that horse so Jackson agreed. At the next big show, the woman entered the horse, rode one go-round and then was disqualified for riding a horse that belonged to Jackson. She had bought and paid for the animal, but had not sent in the transfers; she had entered without the proper documentation."

"Now they're both in trouble," Bert interjected quickly, running his hand through his gray hair.

"But he didn't know anything about it?" Alexandria said, less a question than a statement.

"Right." The bejeweled woman stepped in and rolled her eyes. "Then to make it worse, the woman jumped all over the judge who disqualified her, which upped the ante as far as disciplinary procedures go, and then she sued the association and the judge."

"Don't forget the drug test coming back positive, which cost her and Jackson a bundle," Bert added.

"He was suspended for a year, had no real income, couldn't show or train, you understand."

"Now he's back," Bert said as he wrapped his arm around his little wife, "and most of us have a soft spot for him because he never cried or tried to blame anyone. He's back, and we're glad."

Alexandria smiled. "I see."

"If I was looking for a trainer, I'd sure look his way." Then the woman leaned close and whispered, "But I'd stay far away from that Trisha Wolcott."

"She was the client?" Alexandria asked without really having to. Lots of things made sense now. She'd wondered why a good trainer like Jackson had so few clients.

"Enough, Mabel." Bert finally put his foot down. "Don't be spreading dirt."

She looked to him, brows knit in a dark frown. "Dirt's only dirt when it's not true."

Alexandria sensed now was the time to quit. "I can't tell you how much I appreciate your honesty."

"Well, you give your business to him, you'll never be sorry. Stick around for the finals. Most of us are rooting for him to win the open."

"Thanks, I might do that." Alexandria watched the couple climb to the mezzanine level and disappear in the crowd. She sat back down. They were a cute couple. They were a fit and complemented each other. They belonged together. Once she had thought that she and Jackson fit, but here, now, Alex felt as if she were looking in from a distance. Any relationship between Jackson and her except a business one had been doomed from the beginning. They were two very different people from two very different worlds, and although it had been a pleasant interlude, it couldn't have gone on forever.

But what did go on forever in life? Certainly not the good things. Flowers wilted and died, sunshine left you to darkness every day, and all life ended. Why should she think that what they shared would continue? Losing was part of life; surely she had learned that lesson when she lost her mother or when her father left home all those times she'd begged him to stay.

She looked out over the arena. The bleachers were empty. Cows were gone, as were horses and riders. Even the tractor was gone, and while there were single sounds of life somewhere along the commercial booths in the mezzanine, she was alone. *Better get used to it*, she thought to herself. *Better get back to believing there's only one person in the world who—*

Suddenly she was aware that there was someone behind her. She turned in her seat and saw him. Standing tall on the steps, he looked even more rugged and daring than she remembered. He was braced for a fight.

"You've got no right to be here."

His eyes were full of rage and his face faceted by lines drawn by anger. It took her a moment to realize what he'd said.

"I beg your pardon?"

"Don't beg anything from me, just leave. You've done enough. Leave Everett alone." He ground out each word, then turned and began to climb the stairs.

She jumped to her feet. "Just a minute. You haven't got a clue what's in my mind, but I'm going to tell you."

He stopped and turned to her. "Go ahead, but try to stick to the truth this time."

It felt as if a knife hit and twisted in her gut, but years of training kicked in and she hid it well. "*If* I wanted to see Everett, it would be none of your business. *And* I have every right to come here, to a public gathering, and watch a sports event. I even rooted for you and Everett in the final go, but you can bet I had no intention of ever going near either one of you again."

"At this point, I suppose you've been lying so much, you can't tell it from truth."

She set her purse down and pointed to him, like a lecturing teacher. "I'm damn tired of you calling me a liar. The *truth* is I don't owe you any explanations. I paid you for everything you gave me and that was it."

Something unrecognizable flitted across his face, something that stayed in his eyes a little longer, but disappeared before she could identify it. "I told you it was a business deal right from the start," she added, losing the strength to continue.

He stood still glaring, but the longer he listened to her, the harder it got to breathe. She was beautiful. That night in Temecula her hair wasn't bound up; it was free and falling over her shoulders. Her lips had trailed over his, leaving tracks of electric sensations. He swallowed.

"I don't know how we both got so…"

"It was all a mistake. We need to agree that everything was a mistake," she prompted. "It was an unfortunate daydream, but none of this would ever have worked."

Jackson's heart pounded in his chest. "I made the payment," he said, trying to remain angry when he saw the pain in her eyes. "I want to make sure Paul doesn't screw it up."

"I'll see to it. I *am* a fair person, Jackson. Even if I don't do things the way you would, I am not into cheating people."

Bringing Everett into the picture again rekindled his anger. "I suppose you were going to level with Everett that you wanted Rawlins and that getting close to me had nothing to do with it."

"Let's not even get into that, Jackson. It's too complicated to explain. Just leave it that I'm not interested in Rawlins, at any price, and never will be."

"Then why are you here?"

She couldn't tell him she'd come because she missed everything. The horses, the thrill of a good go, the people—and him. She'd come to be near something he loved, she'd come in the hopes of seeing him, of watching the poetry he wrote as he worked. "To be honest," she cringed as she lied, "I did come here to talk to Everett, but I've changed my mind. Like I said, I'm not interested in Rawlins anymore. You have my word on it."

"Fine," he growled. "Well, fine." He started to turn away but something held him. "I'd like Paul to send some kind of acknowledgment that the balloon is paid in full." He kept looking at her, hoping she'd say something, but she only nodded in silence.

He turned and climbed the stairs where he disappeared beyond the commercial booths. "Never would have worked," she whispered. "Never." Her legs were jelly and her heart felt like it was going to explode. She sat down. "But I do love you, Jackson Morgan."

CHAPTER 11

Jackson stomped back to the stall where he had left the little palomino saddled. Somehow there was no satisfaction in telling her to stay away from Everett, and certainly none in seeing her again. He jerked the saddle from the horse's back and threw it in the stall serving as a tack room. Muttering that he wished he'd never met Alexandria Payne, he grabbed a brush and gave a good imitation of brushing the horse, except that he never moved from the same place on the glossy neck.

"Whoa there, fella," a familiar drawl caught him from behind. "If you scrub that particular spot much more, it'll be shiny and bald."

Jackson exhaled, laid his arm across the palomino's back, and rested his forehead on it.

"You look like a man who's mad enough to kick his own dog."

In answer to Everett, Jackson straightened, shook his head, and threw the brush like a wild pitch into the tack room. "She's here."

Everett hung his head as he propped a hip against the stall door. "Guess I don't need to ask who 'she' is, and it's just another guess that you had words with her."

Tearing at the knot tethering the palomino, Jackson replied, "Stop guessing. And I don't want to talk about it."

"OK. I can see that you want to bury it."

He led the horse into the closest stall, removed the halter, and came out. "That's right, I don't want to talk about her at all." He latched the door. "Do you know why she was here?"

Everett got about half a shake of his head before Jackson started in again.

"I'll tell you why. She came here to talk you out of Rawlins, that's why. She's still manipulating and lying, that's why."

Jackson stomped back to the tack room and hung the halter. When he came out, Everett began.

"She didn't come here to talk to me about Rawlins."

Jackson shot a pitying glance out of the corner of his eye as he closed the padlock on the tack room latch. "Give me a break. She told me that's why she was here."

He started walking and Everett stood, thumbs in his pockets, waiting to see what reaction his words would have. "She's lying."

Jackson stomped on.

"I gave her Rawlins on the condition she'd never bother you again."

Jackson stopped short. "You what?"

"The last contract I sent her was a gift. I told her Rawlins was hers, for nothing. All she had to do was stay out of your life." He shifted and sauntered toward the younger man, whose puzzled look only deepened. "She was lying if she said she was here to see me about it, cuz she already turned it down, flat."

Everett strolled past Jackson, who seemed unable to move, and was quite a way ahead of him when he called out, halting the older man.

"Then why would she lie now?"

Everett turned and smiled. "Because, young feller, I think the woman does actually love you."

Jackson was speechless, but he found himself walking like a robot to Everett's side and then following his lead while deep in thought. They ended up at Everett's truck where he again imitated every move and got inside.

"Why are you on her side all of a sudden? Why is she pure gold now and not before?"

"No one said she had wings and a halo, but I'll tell you this. When I looked into her background in the very beginning, all I saw was a barracuda. She went after anything she wanted and got it, no matter what. She and that partner of hers are pretty well known for being unbeatable in business, and if she was hunting your head, it was pretty certain she'd come up with it sooner or later."

As Everett pulled out into Ogden traffic, Jackson settled into his seat. "You told me all that before; what's changed your mind? I know it wasn't me."

"Nope. I thought you were so infatuated with her that I wouldn't have believed much you told me about her. Besides, I figured she could lead you anywhere."

"Don't give me any compliments. You make me sound like a snot-nosed kid who just had his first kiss."

"Don't get me wrong, Jackson, but I've known you ever since you *were* a snot-nosed kid, and that's precisely why I knew when you finally fell in love, it was going to be a forever thing. I just wanted to make sure the woman felt the same way. To begin with, I didn't think Alex—"

"Now wait a minute." Jackson turned sideways in his seat. "You're trying to manipulate my life worse than she is. I feel like a horse running uphill with hobbles on. I am trying, but I can't seem to get up any speed because you're hanging on to one ankle and she's around the other."

Everett pulled into the Hilton parking lot. As soon as the engine was turned off, Jackson got out. "Just leave me alone for a while. Both of you." He slammed the truck door.

Everett watched the man who would inherit everything he had stride across the parking lot and go into the motel. "I suspect you'll be doing a lot of thinking, son. Maybe I shouldn't have interfered, but you'll have to chalk it up to an old man trying to help. Yep, you're a stubborn son-of-a-gun. You wouldn't take my money, and I have to chase you down and beat you with advice before you'll take it, but I have to try."

Later he called Jackson's room, but there was no answer. Dinnertime rolled around and there was still no sign of him. Everett wasn't worried, but he knew Jackson needed to focus on tomorrow's finals. He was sitting good in every class and had a chance to win it all. The money would do him good, but the publicity would do him better.

Jackson needn't have worried. The next day every ride he turned in was golden. He turned in scores most people only dream about, and when the pictures were all taken and the celebrating began, Jackson was the top dog, the Open Champion. Everett kept an eye peeled all day for Alexandria, in case she might still be around, but never located her.

The owners of the horses Jackson had showed to perfection planned a spur-of-the-moment dinner party, and he and about forty people paraded through the T.G.I. Friday's. Jackson was jubilant and satisfied that he'd come back the right way, with hard work, talent, and good horse flesh. Beer, whiskey, and wine flowed freely, and toast after toast loosened Jackson's normally reserved demeanor.

Suddenly, amid the ribald celebration, a wave of melancholy washed over him. He saw Trisha sitting by herself in the corner and felt sorry for her. Not because she was on the fringes of the fun, but because she was alone and because he knew how that particular ache grew inside a person until it was overwhelming and debilitating.

He rose from his seat, grabbing his drink as he went toward her.

"Can I sit down?"

She looked up, wary and defensive. "I suppose you can sit anywhere you want to. It's your party." She took a long drink and drained the last of her scotch. "I'd like another," she ordered as the barmaid passed. "How about you, Jackson? Can I buy you a drink? It's the least I can do for the man who rode my horse to victory."

"No thanks," he said, as somber as a turkey on Thanksgiving Day. "I just thought you looked like you could use a little company."

"Don't you dare pity me, Jackson. I can hear it in your voice and I don't want it. Do you understand?"

He leaned back and laughed. "What a pair we are. We both have everything we ever wanted but no one to share it with."

"What do you mean? Look at all these people here. They're your family; they love you, Jackson. And then tell me there's one of them that even likes me." She nodded and took a swallow of his drink. "Yuck, watered-down whiskey." She then giggled. "At least you don't drink wine like all those other pansies."

She propped her elbow on the table and rested her cheek in her hand and looked at him. "We would have made a great pair, Jackson Morgan. But I blew it, didn't I?"

He smiled. "It just didn't happen with us, Trisha. But there is someone out there who will fit the bill for you."

"Just like there's someone out there for you, right, Jackson?"

He nodded. "That's right. There is someone out there for me."

"Alexandria," she said as she nodded, helplessly lost in scotch. "She's the one. I could see it the first time I saw you together. It just made me mad that you found someone and I didn't."

He sat forward. "How come everyone is falling over themselves now, telling me she's the one when before—"

"She's the one." Trisha licked her lips and tipped his chin with her thumb and forefinger, as if she were preparing for a kiss. "It's written in your eyes."

He swept her hand from his face. "I think you've had too much to drink. You're seeing things."

Trisha had a few more things to say, but Jackson's mind was stuck on the phrase "she's the one." From that point on, he heard only scattered bits and pieces of the party around him. The waitress brought Trisha's drink and he took her hand in his. "Well, the coach is about to turn into a pumpkin and I have to get up early to load up horses and get home."

He kissed her hand, then stood.

"Find me a prince, Jackson. If I can't have you, then who's second best?" Trisha's pouty red lips and her delicate features would have demanded a second look from any man, but he knew what she really needed was a man to see beyond them, to the lost little girl who was calling out for love.

"Hey, young fella, why haven't I seen you out there with all your friends?" Everett walked up behind him.

"Ev. Your timing is perfect. This lady is in dire need of a Prince Charming, and I can't think of anyone better suited to fit the bill than you." He pulled Covington to his side. "Trisha, this is Everett Covington. Now I know you've met, but tonight you are strangers. Trisha is looking for—" He blushed as he scanned her face. "Well, like I said, she's been jilted and she needs someone who can make her forget her troubles. Everett, on the other hand, is a man among men and he..." Jackson looked into the older man's eyes. "He's good at picking up strays and showing them what life is all about."

Trisha giggled and Everett sat down beside her as Jackson backed away. Too bad life wasn't a fairy tale where everything turned out happily ever after. Calling over the crowd to say goodbye, he turned and went out the door to the parking lot. When he turned the corner, he surprised a couple who had been kissing in the shadows. It seemed like love was all around him but just beyond his grasp. All the way to the motel, the feeling grew that maybe he was wrong. That maybe he'd really screwed up.

It had been so good for such a short time. He had loved her and he'd thought she loved him.

He got into bed and turned off the light. He wanted her in bed next to him. He wanted the feel of her hand as it brushed across his body and he wanted the sound of her whispering his name as they lay entwined between the sheets, bodies glistening with the glow of passion.

So what was wrong? Why wasn't she here with him?

It was simple. He wanted not only her body but her soul. If she didn't really love him, then she didn't belong in his heart, in his soul, in his bed.

He'd gone back to the arena to try to find her the day before, but she was gone. There were things he wanted to know, like why she lied to him about being there to see Everett, and every time he thought about her, there were more questions he wanted answered. Not the least of which, now that he'd thought about it, was: Did she love him or not?

Jackson pulled the sheet close to his chin and rolled on his side. In fetal position, the reality of what he contemplated hit him. He loved Alex. It would be just like him to go straight to her and ask if she really loved him, but then he'd get an answer and there would no longer be any doubt.

He did love her.

What if she told him he'd been a passing fancy? That what she told him was love had been nothing more than infatuation? What would he do then, if he admitted now that she was part of him? Would he live a solitary and pathetic existence as Trisha did, taking out her misery on people around her?

What if Alex said she could live without him?

The next morning the wake-up call rang, and instead of the usual automated version, an operator told him there was a message for him. The caller said it was important that it get to Jackson before he checked out.

The voice mail message was from Everett, who said it was late, he was returning the favor, and had found out where Alex was staying. Ironically, she was at the Hilton, the same place they were. "Just in case," he'd said before he told him to drive carefully on the way home.

Jackson sat up, swung his legs to the floor, and rubbed his eyes. The introduction to Trisha must have been the favor, and "just in case" was his not-so-subtle prod. Now was his chance. She was here and he could ask all the questions he wanted. Before he had the chance to talk himself out of it, he picked up the phone and asked for her room.

It rang so many times he was sure she'd already gone, but suddenly she said hello, and he was hard pressed to squeeze out a single word.

"Hi." A long silence followed and he thought she might be preparing to hang up, so he began, somewhat feebly. "Alex? I wondered if you'd come have breakfast with me?"

Another pregnant pause before she finally answered. "I'll have coffee with you, but I need to be getting to the airport."

"Fine. Downstairs at the coffee shop in fifteen minutes?"

"OK."

The connection broke and Jackson found himself as breathless as if he'd just run a mile.

Only fifteen minutes—holy mackerel, why hadn't he given himself more time? He jumped out of bed and sprinted to the bathroom, turned on the shower, got in, got out, and dried off. He checked his watch. *Five minutes left*. He had to hurry. What if he was late and she left? He pulled on socks, pants, and boots. He grabbed a shirt; better button up and tuck it in on the run.

He got to the elevators just in time to see the doors close on a down car. He pushed the button frantically, hoping another was close. By the time he'd finished with the buttons, the bell rang, and he stood in front of the doors with unzipped pants, tucking in his shirt.

The door opened and two women, one gray and the other graying, greeted him with wide eyes.

"Sorry, my girl is waiting downstairs." He stuffed the tail in and tried to smooth it. "I'm going to ask her to marry me."

They snickered between them, and by the time the elevator reached the ground floor, they were checking him out.

"You've got a fly-away hank of hair," one said as the door opened.

"Thanks," he said as looked at his watch and leaped from the elevator.

"Good luck," called out the gray-haired woman as he rounded the corner.

Jackson trotted the long concourse, dodging people until he was almost to the coffee shop. He slowed to a fast walk. Fourteen minutes. He slowed even more. She wasn't there. He had a clear view of the entrance, and she was nowhere to be found.

His mind began backtracking. He'd been a fool to say fifteen minutes. Alex never got ready for anything in fifteen minutes. She'd probably agreed just so he'd have to wait. He sauntered to the hostess and she waved him in.

"The lady is waiting for you." She pointed toward the back, and he saw Alexandria sitting, waiting.

He walked closer, his heart beating, a slight sweat breaking out on his forehead that could have been from the sprint to get there or from nervousness—he didn't know which.

She wasn't smiling, and that unnerved him completely. He remembered the tone of their last encounter and whatever courage he had evaporated like mist on a hot day.

The minty-green business suit she wore made her skin look more bronzed than ever, and although her hair was wound behind her head, the front was soft around her face. He walked to the edge of the table, feeling as awkward as a pup on its first excursion across the lawn.

"Have a seat," she said, all business. "As I said, I have to get to the airport."

He pulled a chair out and sat down. "It's your plane, it'll wait."

Her brows rose and she started to say something, but he cut her off. "Alex, I want to start over."

"It would be nice if we could undo things that didn't go well." She sipped from her cup. "But unfortunately that's not always possible."

"I think it is in this case." He leaned forward to look directly into her blue eyes. "We owe it to ourselves—"

"I'm not sure where this is headed. If you are going to call me a liar again"—her business cool began to heat up—"I'd rather end it right now."

She put both hands on the table and started to stand, but Jackson put his hand over hers. "No, please. Wait," he said, panic creeping in. "I don't know how to start, but I do know I have things to say, things that should have been cleared up a long time ago. I swear I won't say anything about lies. Just sit down." His eyes pleaded with her. "Please."

Slowly she sank to her chair. He hated the deer-in-the-headlights look that she was trying to cover up.

"So far we've been honest, we've been angry, we've been curious, and we've been partners. The one thing we haven't been is friends." He released her hand and plucked a carnation from the bud vase in the center of the table. "I want to be able to hand you a flower and know you won't throw it back at me."

She smiled, her shoulders relaxed, and she took the bloodred flower.

"There's so much we don't know about each other because we've been intent upon setting up a protective shield. Just now it struck me that we need to find out just who is sitting across the table so we can be friends."

"It sounds good, but I don't think it's going to work. We are so different," she argued, sadness in her eyes.

"No. Trust me on this, Alex. I think it's what we need."

On hearing her nickname, she twisted in her chair, as if she were taking a deep seat on a rank bronc. "All right. Go for it. Where do you want to start?"

"I want to start with pancakes and eggs."

"What? I told you I have to—"

"Relax." He waved to the waitress. "The airplane is yours, I told you. I think I'm making progress and I can't stop now."

"I'll have pancakes and scrambled eggs, she'll have toast and orange juice," he told the waitress with Coke-bottle glasses.

"No," Alexandria was going to protest, but she saw the determination on his face and knew it was useless. "OK. Now we're having breakfast. What next?"

"Next," he said, leaning back, suddenly feeling things were beginning to go well, "I want you to tell me how you got to be one of the world's foremost corporate raiders."

She blushed and he laughed.

"That's according to Ev, who, by the way, told me he tried to give you Rawlins."

"But I didn't—"

"Don't change the subject. Back to the question at hand, Madam Chairperson. How?"

She eyed him slyly before she answered. "I lived with board meetings and profit and loss all my life. My father brought the most influential people in the world home, and over dinner I listened to financial schemes that worked and ones that failed. I learned how to bargain and how to see what the bottom line was at an early age, and when I graduated, naturally I fell into the business. Besides," she added, her face becoming a series of hard lines, "the only way to get my father to recognize me was to beat him at his own game."

Looking at Jackson, she was surprised that there was not even a hint of revulsion in his expression. "Go on," he said. "Did you beat him?"

Taking a deep breath she hesitated while the waitress set down a plate heaped with pancakes and eggs and her own smaller plate of toast. "Yes," she said softly after the waitress left. "I did. But it was no victory. It just meant that I was good at what I was doing."

Jackson heard the wounds reopened and wanted to hold her, to reassure her, but she changed the subject.

"And you? Where did you meet Everett?"

"I was sixteen years old and I had been jumping rail cars all over, looking for someplace to belong. I got off in Abilene and stole the keys to the fanciest truck I'd ever seen."

"Everett's truck?" she laughed.

"Yep." He snickered at how stupid he'd been. "Long story short, I bashed up a front fender, and when I got caught, he told the judge, who was a friend of his, that he wanted me to work the damage off. At first I tried to be tough, but before long, he had me eating out of his hand, just like everyone else."

"That's when he put you on a horse, right?" she said, entertained and interested.

"Right." His eyes sparkled and made his face light up. "I found out I was good at it, when I'd never been good at anything else in my life, and it felt so right that I never went back."

"I know how that feels," she said, excitement building. "It's a power trip."

He directed his gaze to her, halted by the tone of her voice. "Is it power to belong?"

The conversation suddenly changed; she was instantly aware and afraid. Everything had gone along comfortably, polite conversation lulling raw nerves, easing bruised feelings, but one or two words later, and it was getting uncomfortably hot and the air was stifling. His penetrating gaze seemed to cut right through her.

"Belonging? No, belonging is not a power trip." She brought her napkin to her mouth and shifted nervously.

"Then what is it?"

"Really, Jackson, how should I know? I've never belonged in my whole life. I—"

"You belong with me, Alex."

How could he sound so horribly calm when she was about to explode, and how could he say such ridiculous things?

"No. I don't even want to talk about it." She thought about leaving, but was sure he'd make a scene. Her only hope was to regain control. "Tell me about the thing with Trisha."

"I thought we were going to be honest with each other."

Her temper flared. "Are you going to call me a liar again?"

"No."

There was a pregnant pause for quite a while, and Alexandria knew she'd hit her mark. He crossed his arms over his chest like an Indian war chief. She'd made him be quiet for the moment, but didn't know if she had it in her to do it again.

"Trisha thought she was in love with me. I was giving her riding lessons and it gradually got away from both of us. She bought a horse from me and together we both were disciplined by the cutting horse association. I wasn't allowed to earn money within the association for a year. At the time, I had just bought my place and had a ten-thousand-dollar balloon payment hanging over my head, and no way to pay it since I was fined and had to go to court. When you came along, it was perfect timing."

Cups rattled around them, distant chatter filled the room, but neither Jackson nor Alexandria moved.

"Why didn't Everett lend you the money?" she whispered as she toyed with the corner of her napkin.

"He offered. But I've never been a man to let others bail me out." He put both palms on the table and leaned forward. "Which is why I'm here now. I love you, Alex, and there's got to be some way we can get through all this chafe and get down to the basic facts."

He reached across the table and touched her chin with his forefinger. She wouldn't look at him, so he gently directed her face to him. "I said I love you. Do you love me, Alex?"

It was impossible to lie at this point, and she tried to avert her gaze but he held her. "I…I don't know," she said on the verge of nervous laughter or tears, whichever might come first.

"You knew in Temecula. Was it a lie?"

She pulled away. "No," she whispered, barely audible to herself. "No, it was no lie." She took a deep breath, her pulse pounding in her temple and her hands shaking even though she held one tight in the other. One tear escaped and dropped to her cheek. "I do love you."

Again he tenderly tipped her chin so he could see her face. "Then why the tears? We love each other. It's good news."

"No, I keep trying to tell you, it's not." She burst out in tears as she got up and ran from the restaurant.

Jackson leaped up, reached for her as she ran by, and missed by mere inches. He ran into the spectacled waitress, who wanted to know if he wanted the bill added to his room charge.

"Yes, 2218," he said as he charged past her. Outside there was no sign of Alexandria, and he hastily concluded that if he were a crying woman he'd head for his room. He ran again through the concourse and found her waiting by the elevators.

"Now I know we have something to talk about," he said as he took her by the elbow. "Your room or mine?"

"Neither. This won't work. There's no use in talking about it; it just won't work."

"Wrong." He stepped into the elevator, taking her with him. "My room."

Alexandria fought with herself. She didn't want to go to his room, but she didn't want him in hers because there would be no place for her to run to. Like an unwilling horse, it felt like he dragged her every step until they reached 2218. He produced a key and they entered. Once inside, she knew she had to compose herself, knowing that things weren't going to get easier, just more impossible.

His bed was unmade, and it brought unwelcome thoughts of what might have been. It would have been great, but she had to reconcile herself to the fact that memories were all she was going to have.

He stood in front of the door like an Egyptian guard, legs akimbo and arms crossed. Everything about him, down to his expression, was strong and unyielding. She began to doubt she had the courage to walk away from a confrontation with him. The only thing that made her speak first was the fact that he would not. It was a proven negotiating tactic, and she approved of his approach, even though it put her at a decided disadvantage.

"Stop thinking with your heart and start thinking for a minute with your head. You and I have nothing in common other than a month together. You've gone back to your own life and I've gone back to mine. There's no place for me with you, and I know you'd die living in the city with me, not to mention the fact that you'd be harping at me all the time about my ethics." She'd spoken as quickly as she could to give him no opportunity to interrupt, and at the end, she wanted to gasp for breath. She felt light-headed and sick to her stomach, and she reached for the back of a chair to steady herself. "So you see, it won't work. There has to be something more."

He continued to stand, looking over her like a stone sentinel.

"Why aren't you saying anything? I thought you'd..." Her voice died out as she suspected a trap. "You aren't going to let me out of here, are you?"

"Don't be ridiculous."

His gravelly voice gave her shivers. "Then what are you going to do?"

"I don't know." His great body seemed to soften with each word. "I honestly don't know. I've never loved a woman like you before, and I've never had to fight like this just to be heard. I'm a little embarrassed, but I'm more worried that you won't listen."

"I'm sorry, but you don't understand."

He moved toward her as the words tumbled out. "It's you who doesn't understand."

She backed away from him, but he advanced quickly and took her in his arms. There was no hope if she gave in now and she struggled to be free. He let her go, but held her wrist. Slowly he drew her forward until his lips touched hers. His kiss was gentle, forgiving, and unbearable.

Alexandria knew she should run, but the knowledge that this was probably the last time he would ever kiss her made her stop to relish the feeling.

"Please," she said as she finally pushed him away. "Please, I can't think at all."

He covered her mouth once again to silence her, but pulled away slowly. "It's your choice, Alex." His gruff whisper was thickened by passion. "Do you want me to stop?"

Alex was unable to think, much less answer, for what seemed like an eternity. Finally she mouthed the words she couldn't bear to speak aloud. "Yes."

Slowly he relieved the pressure and she felt him release her wrist. She couldn't look at him, but she knew he was watching.

"OK." He stepped back. "I'll do anything you say. You tell me what's next."

"Please, Jackson, you've got to try to understand how impossible this is. We're not Romeo and Juliet; we're not love-stricken teenagers; we are adults who have responsibilities." Her eyes began to cloud with tears and she tried to hold them back. "This is not a fairy tale, and we've got to realize that when it comes down to everyday life—after the chemistry cools off—we have to go on living. I want to remember how sweet it was for us, not live in fear you'll leave me when the illusion is gone."

"Alex." He touched her cheek; she realized he was wiping the tears that had begun to roll down.

Quickly she waved his hand away and looked straight at him to make sure there was no mistake. "My name is Alexandria. I live in Los Angeles, and I'm a corporate raider. I have to go now or I'll miss the appointments I have scheduled."

She turned and opened the door. As she stepped into the hall, she looked back. She'd never seen such pain on his face.

"Please forgive me, Jackson, I *do* love you, but this has to be good-bye."

CHAPTER 12

"For Christ's sake, son, I never thought I'd see you give up on something you wanted." Everett had been arguing with Jackson for the last half hour and showed no sign of giving in. Jackson, on the other hand, felt like he'd been ridden hard and put up wet. At least he was sitting on the couch and comfortable.

"Ev, come on, you're always the one who says a man has to cut his losses. This has gone bad and I see it. There's no reason to continue chasing after her."

"I can't believe I'm hearing this kind of stuff from you. When I jerked you out of the penal system, you'd never heard the word *quit*. That's why you kept gettin' back on that miserable black horse. He'd buck you off, and you'd go right back for more. Why do you think I called him Joker?"

Jackson rolled his eyes as he answered. "You told me a hundred times, because the horse had enough cow and the breeding to be a world champion, but he never found a rider who made him want to do anything but joke about the subject. I know, but this is different. I had a chance then. Alex has told me over and over there's not a snowball's chance in hell that we're goin' to make it. She won't even let me call her Alex—it's Alexandria, and probably the next time I see her it will be back to Ms. Payne."

"So?"

Jackson toyed with the table lamp next to him, pulling the chain and turning it on and then off. “So I’m not making any progress.”

“What makes you think so?”

“She keeps running away from me, that’s why.”

“Doesn’t a person run away from things that scare ’em?”

“Ev, I don’t know anymore.”

“Well, think about it. You sound tired, son, and it’s late. You go try to get some sleep. I’m going to Amarillo tomorrow, but I’ll call you when I get back. Go sleep, you hear me?”

“I will,” Jackson lied. He hadn’t been able to sleep the night through for a week since Ogden. “Talk to you later.” He hesitated, knowing how worried Everett was to have called every day for the last three days. “And Ev, thanks.”

He hung the phone up and pulled the string on the lamp one last time. Darkness settled around him like a shroud and he was alone again. It used to be the way he liked it, but now it felt like punishment. Being alone was oppressive when all he wanted was the sound of her voice, the ripple of her laughter, the flash in her eyes when he pushed her to ride a little harder.

He got up from the couch and went to the bedroom, but as soon as he touched the threshold, he stopped. Like a shrine, her things were still there, waiting for her return, and suddenly he didn’t want to see physical proof that she was gone. He closed the door, turned, and went outside. He walked down to the pasture in back of the barn where Joker was.

The old horse was in the far corner by the huge oak trees as usual, but since there was no moon, Jackson couldn’t actually see him until he was very close, but a soft nicker welcomed him.

“Hey, old man. Here I am again, needing you, wanting advice.” He ran his hand through the thick mane and felt the familiar nuzzling that meant he understood. “I’ve never been in such a fix. I don’t know if I’d love her as much if she was an easy catch, but it doesn’t matter; I have no choice and don’t think

I ever did. I guess I should have known when someone named Hesperia called that something extraordinary was happening." He ran his hand along the horse's top line and down into his tail. A couple of open-handed pats and he wandered to the base of the oak, sat down, and rested against it.

"You should see her ride, Joker. She's got more natural talent than I ever hoped to have, and I can see it in her face that it excites her; she likes it. I just can't figure why she's throwing it all away."

Joker's arthritic joints creaked and popped as he turned and moved close enough to put his head right in front of Jackson, who rubbed his broad forehead. "Sure, she's used to caviar and jet airplanes, but she was happy here, I know. It showed like a neon light."

The gelding inhaled, then exhaled as if he had seen it too. "Maybe it's all me. I didn't trust her when I should have, but darn it, Joker, she wasn't straight with me."

Joker blew his nose, and in that unique way a horse has of making its point, he blew dirt and wet things all over Jackson. "I take it you don't agree," he said as he wiped his arms and chest. "Well, it doesn't matter much now, we both made mistakes." Joker shook his head, probably to fend off evening flies, but it looked for all the world like he was agreeing with Jackson.

For a long time, they both were quiet. Joker was probably sleeping, like an old man dozes in his recliner at night, but all sorts of things were going through Jackson's mind. Was she afraid, as Everett concluded? Her reluctance to deal with the truth meant she was afraid of...he tried to plug in a number of things, but it always came back to the same thing. She didn't want things to change. She *was* enjoying cutting, life on the ranch, and him. Her fear grew from the fact that she believed things would change. She was afraid she would lose something that meant a lot to her.

"She said she loves me, you know."

Joker nodded in agreement.

"She never lied to me about that."

Joker nodded again.

"She only lied when she was afraid." It flashed back to him that she lied when she told him she'd come to Ogden to see Everett, and suddenly he saw the barracuda, the financial genius, as a vulnerable woman, one who had to succeed in order to get her own father to pay attention to her, one who had taken a cold fish like Paul Maitland into her arms because she was starved for warmth.

Suddenly he knew what he had to do. He'd once called her Rapunzel and urged her to let down her hair. Now she'd done it and it was his turn to climb the tower and set her free. She was waiting for him to slay her dragons and all he'd been thinking about was slaying his own.

He stood so fast that Joker blew rollers and momentarily shied away. Jackson hugged the sleek neck. "Joker, you're perfect. I've never had a problem that you didn't help with, but now I've gotta go."

It was a clear day, clearer than most in Los Angeles. Jackson had caught a red-eye and although he'd hadn't slept at all, he wasn't tired; in fact, he'd never felt so alive, so invigorated. APM owned and was housed in a huge building that cast its distinctive silhouette across the downtown LA skyline. It hadn't been hard to find, even for a man more comfortable with rolling hills and creeks than city blocks and taxicabs.

Jackson paused in front of a giant carved mahogany door on the twenty-seventh floor of a twenty-eight story building. He didn't know if she was in this early, but finding her was the first step of his plan. The door wasn't as heavy as it looked, and he stepped inside. The air was cool, but he knew beads of nervous perspiration were about to garnish his temple as he stepped up to a very contemporary receptionist's desk. A pretty brunette was on the phone; she looked to him as soon as he came in, then went back to the phone call.

Jackson waited while she finished, hung up, and directed her attention to him. "Hesperia?" he asked doubtfully.

"Ah, no." The receptionist smiled as if he'd just made an off-color joke. "She's Ms. Payne's personal secretary. May I help you?"

"Is Ms. Payne in?"

"Do you have an appointment?"

"No, but—"

"Then I'll have to check. May I tell her who's calling?"

"No."

She looked to him, her expression a direct question of his stability and intentions. "I have to know who—"

"Just tell me if she's in, please."

The woman hesitated, then lifted the phone. "There's a man here to see Ms. Payne, and he won't give his name." Her voice was tentative.

A door to the left opened and Paul appeared. "Just as I thought," he said as he glided toward Jackson. "Mr. Morgan, why are you here?"

"I don't remember asking to see you." Jackson stood his ground, knowing that if he had to fight for her, he would.

Paul rubbed his hands together as he walked toward the entrance door. He grabbed the handle and pulled it open. "You have no reason to see *her*, either. I suggest you leave right now."

Jackson drew a deep breath. "No, Paul. I have to see Alex, and if I have to camp out here, I'm going to do it." He made a show of looking around until he spied the leather couch. "I'm used to sleeping on the couch"—he went over and seated himself, bouncing a little to test the quality—"and this will be fine." He flicked imaginary lint from his pants then crossed his arms and settled back. "I'd sure like a cup of coffee if you have one."

"You won't have time to finish it."

"Then she's here? I won't have to wait that long?"

Paul let go of the door and walked closer. "Morgan, she doesn't want to see you. Why don't you leave her alone? Haven't you hurt her enough?"

He stood, as tall as Maitland, but fifty pounds heavier than the wispy blond in the Armani suit. "I'll leave after I've seen Alex, and it's none of your business why I'm here."

"*Alexandria* and I are partners. Anything you can say to her, you can say to me."

As the two stood nose to nose, inches from igniting a direct confrontation, the mahogany door opened and a very prim-looking woman with a tight little bun walked in, arms loaded with file folders—some of which were about to escape.

Thinking quickly, Jackson smiled and walked to her. "Can I carry anything?"

"Well, yes, thank you."

"No, he can't help," Paul shouted, standing with his fists doubled at his sides like a child about to throw a tantrum.

"Hesperia?" Jackson asked as he took the majority of the folders, certain she could be no other.

"Yes?" she answered as she glanced between the two men.

"I'd like to see Alex. Is she in?"

Hesperia looked to Paul whose head went from side to side in a decisive *no*.

She looked back to Jackson, smiled, and said, "Yes. Follow me." She and Jackson went through the door on the right and left Paul sputtering in the receptionist's area. Hesperia dumped her few files on a cluttered desk, motioning for Jackson to do the same. "She's been here working all night, Mr. Morgan, and… well, you can go right in."

Very prim and proper, she sat down at her desk and, without looking up, suggested, "Take off your cowboy hat. You don't want her to think you're ill mannered."

Suddenly Jackson was nervous as a prostitute in church. There was no longer any doubt that he was sweating bullets and his pulse was a hundred times the normal rate. He swept the Stetson from his head, glad he'd brought it instead of the straw, and stepped to the door.

He cleared his throat. Was this insanity? Should he leave now, before someone got hurt? *No.* This was going to keep them from being hurt. He grabbed the doorknob, twisted, and forged ahead.

Inside, he saw her bent over her desk, head down, directing all her attention to what she was writing. "Just put them over there, Hesperia. I'll go through them when I have time."

"It's not Hesperia," he said, suddenly not so sure she was the one who needed rescuing.

Alexandria looked up and stood, tapping her pencil absently on the desktop. "What are you doing here?"

His heart was in his throat. How should he begin when she held his whole life in her very capable hands?

"It wasn't a trick question." Her voice wasn't nearly as strong as it had been the first time. "Why did you come?"

"I love you, Alex."

"We've already been through this." He saw her sit quickly and realized her knees were as wobbly as his.

"But we haven't got it right yet." He tossed his hat toward a pair of armchairs and it landed like a Frisbee. "You belong with me."

For all her bravado, it was clear that Alexandria wanted to turn and run. "Look," she said, "my stomach has been ruined by all this, and I haven't slept well for a long time. I just don't know how to make you see that I'm right."

She wasn't going to give up easily, but her hand trembled and suddenly he realized Everett was right. She was petrified. No one had ever stayed with her. Jackson strolled to her desk and leaned forward, placing both palms in front of him and leaning across the wide polished expanse until he was very close. "You're not right. You're afraid to go somewhere you've never been before because you have always hedged your bets and you can't guarantee this one."

She popped up, threw the pencil down, and maneuvered away from him to look out the plate glass window. "I'm not afraid. I just know it wouldn't work, that's all. The kind of love you're talking about is not for me. I want exactly what I've got."

"Maybe you do want what you have now, but you also want more. I'm not saying you have to give up everything you have now; all I'm asking is that you let me in. We're the same kind of people." He moved closer, still speaking to her back. "We're both very good at what we do; we just do different things."

She shook her head, but he continued. "You need me as much as I need you. You need someone to come home to at night who will celebrate your victories with you, you need someone to tell you you're all right when things go wrong." He touched her shoulder and turned her to face him. Tears slowly slid down her cheeks, and it nearly killed him. "You need someone to ride in the moonlight with you and someone to run his fingers through your hair and remind you not to be so stuffy." He dipped to look into her eyes. "You need me."

"No. I don't need—" He silenced her with a single finger over her lips.

"Please, let me finish. In Ogden, I listened while you did the talking, but this time I have a lot to say, and I'm not going to be polite about this. I'm going to talk until I'm done, and even if I have to gag you, you're going to listen."

She started to turn away. "I don't think so—"

He seized her arm and directed her to a chair where he sat her down. He then began walking around the room, wringing his hands, looking at the furnishings as he went. It was all shiny and dust-free. It was sterile; it was not the Alex he knew. He passed behind her. "I don't know why it is that a person has to care for someone before all their faults come to the surface."

"Now I have faults?" She sniffed, mocking him.

"Of course, we all do, but the point is that a man, or a woman, doesn't fall in love until he looks deep inside the other person. About the time he's hopelessly caught, he's deep enough to see the skeletons."

He heard her theatrical sigh. "This isn't sounding like love to me; it sounds like a witch hunt."

He was across the room when he stopped. "What I'm trying to say is I understand now about Rawlins. I'm sorry."

Alexandria looked at him, hands in his pockets, looking for all the world like a little boy.

"Not that you needed it, but I've forgiven everything and I know that I was—"

"An ass?"

Ahh. He was making progress. "Well, maybe not an ass, but a mule for sure. Everett always said I was stubborn." He came to her and sat on the corner of her desk. "If we take out all this business about Everett, Rawlins, and Paul, you have to admit we were very happy for a month."

She pushed back in her chair and rubbed her forehead with one hand. "That's the point. A month is a very short time and then what happens when the Rawlins deals and the Trishas enter the picture again? What then?"

"Then we'll deal with them as they come. We'd both be fools to think we were going to have an argument-free relationship. You talked about reality, but in reality, all couples have disagreements, but"—a sparkle formed in his eyes that lit up his face—"couples get to make up afterwards. No, we aren't going to live a fairy tale, but no one does. There are plenty of flawed relationships, and I don't think ours is as flawed as some. After all, I'm not in jail and you haven't slept with my brother."

"You have a brother?" Alexandria fought it, but a smile crept over her.

"No. Don't change the subject."

"OK," she said, now steady and strong, "but look around. You don't see a horse, a cow, or even grass. You can never be happy here."

He leaned over and lay on his side on her desk, propping his head on his hand. "I'm still not giving up. What I do see is you, and that's all I need. I don't want you to change; all I want you to do is love me."

He was too close. Alexandria was afraid he'd see how close to giving in she was. She wanted him more than anything, but knew she couldn't live through having him leave once she took him into her heart. "I do love you. I've told you that," she said, not giving an inch.

"And that's all we need, Alex. Trust me. Let me handle this. I won't let you down." He sat up, swinging his legs around so that she sat between them. "I promise I won't leave. How could I leave someone who means as much to me as life itself? I've tried every way I know how to win you, but in the end, it's going to be your decision. I know what I want, I always have. It's you, and I think I've been waiting for you ever since I was born. I dreamed at night of someone to take me in her arms and kiss all my worries away and who would make everyday a birthday, someone who would have my kids and who would join me in making *our* home and *our* family." He slid off the desk and drew her up as he stood. "I've kinda been on the outside looking in, just like you have. It's time we shared our dreams."

Shaky knees, trembling hands, quavering voice—she'd never known someone who could promise exactly what she had been dreaming of. "What if all I can be is Alexandria?" she whispered. "What if I can't be all those things?"

"That's the beauty of it all." He gathered her gently in his arms. "You already are."

Alexandria buried her face in his chest, the crisp white shirt feeling so much like home to her. "Don't you ever give up?"

"No. And neither do you. Especially not when it's the most important thing we'll ever do." He tipped her face toward his and caressed her cheek with his thumb. "You have the power, Alex. You decide." His lips brushed her forehead, then roamed over her face until he reached her mouth. The kiss was gentle, loving, and confident.

He pulled back, and she smiled.

"What if I need you to go to New York City with me and wear a tuxedo?"

"I can do it." He kissed her.

She broke away. "What if we have to live down here part time?"

"I'm sure Los Angeles has a place where we can have horses and a helicopter pad." He drew her back to his kiss.

"What if I get crabby and all twisted up about a deal?"

Jackson grinned. "We'll find a way to relieve the tension."

Alex smiled. "I'm not sure how we're going to do this, Jackson, but you win. We can do it." She grabbed his collar and, eager for his touch, brought his lips to hers once again. "I warn you, though, Alex is going to be as hard to satisfy as Alexandria is. I'm hooked on you and those cutting horses, and I'm even going to learn how to back that gigantic horse trailer, I'm—"

"Whoa, there. First things first." He reached behind her and removed her hair clip, then ran his fingers through her hair, fluffing it around her face and neck. He got down on one knee. He took her hand and kissed the back of it.

He looked up to her, opened his mouth, then closed it and swallowed hard. "I don't mind telling you that my heart is thumping like a jumping bean gone wild and I've never been so damned afraid in my life. I've never talked so much or prayed so hard."

"So stop chattering and get to the point."

With a grin as big as Texas, he said, "Will you marry me?"

"What if I want a big formal wedding?"

"You can have anything you want, just marry me."

"What if—"

He stood, scooped her up in his arms, and twirled her around. When he stopped, he grew serious. "Stop asking questions. We're smart people. Together we will figure out a way to make it work. We are both looking for someone to be there for us. Someone to grow old with, someone to remember the good times with, someone to—"

Alex suddenly kissed Jackson. She pulled back and smiled. "Stop talking. The answer is yes. Forever…yes."

The wedding was huge. That was for Alex. It was held outdoors in a field of poppies. That was for Jackson. Her wedding gown was a designer original that cost more than the training bargain that first brought them together. That was most certainly for Alex since all Jackson could think about was taking it off after the ceremony and reception.

He was dressed handsomely in a black tie tuxedo and black felt hat. Alex peeked from the window of the luxury motor home that was her dressing room and wondered once again how she'd ever been lucky enough to have a man like Jackson fall in love with her. She glanced at the guests and laughed to herself. This was the first time she'd had a moment to actually look at what was the beginning of her new life.

Guests on the bride's side were dressed to the nines. Besides her dress, designer clothing stock must have jumped ten points. Everyone from Valentino to Vera Wang was represented. Most were business associates who wouldn't have missed this high-priced social affair for anything. Paul was present with a starlet whose dress revealed way too much cleavage.

The groom's guests were quite another story. From the rear, it looked like a sea of black felt. For every woman dressed sensibly smart, there was at least one man crowned with a Stetson. She shivered. It was perfect. The sight seemed like living proof that their worlds could mesh.

A quiet knock on her door and Hesperia's voice told her it was time. She opened the door and saw the older lady smiling.

"You are radiant," said Hesperia.

Alex stood speechless for a second, then smiled. "You also look wonderful. I am so thankful you agreed to be my matron of honor."

"I can't think of anything more important. Now, you need to emerge from your cocoon so you don't keep that saint of a man waiting any longer."

When the door opened and Alex floated down the stairs onto the white runner leading toward him, Jackson was struck dumb. He heard nothing; he could say nothing. He saw nothing but his angel coming nearer. He knew by the way his heart leaped at the sight of Alex and by the way his body was drawn to her that he had won it all.

Forever was written in her eyes as she reached out for him. Suddenly nervous, he swallowed. Life *would* be good. It would be hot. But there would be no quitting.

Alex smiled. Jackson took her hand and instantly both grew strong. Instantly love sheltered and inspired. Forever began now.

EPILOGUE

Life was good. Alex handed Jackson the bridle for the palomino and kissed him for luck. They were in Fort Worth at the Will Rogers Equestrian Center, and Jackson was one ride from winning the biggest and most prestigious prize the National Cutting Horse Association offered.

"That baby's gonna have some big boots to fill," said Everett as he walked up. "Appears to me that you could fall off in there and still win."

"As long as there are no hot quits, I'm happy." Alex ran her hand across the top of her expanding stomach.

"We don't do hot quits," Jackson said, a gleam in his eye. "One look at that huge belly you have should prove that."

Alex grinned. "You sure are proud of yourself, cowboy."

Jackson nodded as he mounted up. "Yep. I'm a proud man. I've got everything I ever wanted—a wife, a good start on a family, and—"

"And don't forget the most eager godparents-to-be who ever walked the earth."

Alex turned to find Trisha stepping closer to Everett and claiming his arm possessively. If there were miracles in this world, and she knew there were, then the marriage of Everett and Trisha had to be one. From the day Everett took her to dinner and explained how *his* lady would act, she had been a different woman. They had taken vows the month after she and Jackson had, and Alex was certain it would be until death do them part.

Everett, the tough business man, the man's man, loved the way Trisha fawned over him, and Trisha was way more interested in Everett's happiness than she was in spending money. A miracle.

Not that she and Jackson hadn't found their own miracle. The balance between his life and hers had been easier than she had ever thought it would be. Paul had taken over as CEO of APM, and through the modern wonders of computer conference meetings, e-mail, and cell phones, Alexandria's business prowess was as sharp as ever. There was a decided change in her direction as far as ripping and tearing viable businesses, but as soon as Paul found out he still made more money than he could spend, even he agreed to the modifications.

Alex heard the announcer call Jackson to the arena and watched him ride forward. He was the man of her dreams. He was a cowboy in every sense. He lived every day with courage. He usually talked less and said more, and he always finished what he started. He sat tall, proud of who he was and what he did, but the most important thing to Alex was that he loved her.

The cool smell of tanbark and shavings and cows hit her. A sudden and overwhelming sense of comfort and ease struck, and slowly she was mesmerized by the sight of him and the palomino, the sound and the feel of this lone rider working in a huge covered arena as if there was no one and nothing else on earth. It was just as it had been the first time she'd seen him; Jackson was a conductor guiding a symphony orchestra.

He moved easily into the herd, cut out a black baldy, and let the palomino work. Fluid, smooth, and powerful, the team of horse and rider were flawless. Alex never ceased to be impressed while watching Jackson. As strong and powerful as he was, he was the most gentle and caring man she'd ever known.

At the conclusion of his ride, the crowd went wild. There was no doubt that he'd won the cutting as easily as he'd won her heart. Everett whooped beside her. Trisha jumped for joy, and Alex suddenly clutched her belly. The baby kicked in appreciation of the win, and that was the moment that Alex knew, without a doubt, that she was the luckiest woman alive.

The End

ABOUT THE AUTHOR

Photo by Louis Rayor, 2012

A stable manager and business owner, Kathryn Roberts knows her way around both boardrooms and horse barns. This diverse expertise led her to write *Hot Quit*. She has previously published articles as well as two nonfiction guides, *Mounted Training* and *Mounted Search and Rescue*, and is a member of Romance Writers of America. Roberts earned her BS in animal science at California Polytechnic University in San Luis Obispo, where she met her husband. When Roberts isn't busy writing or working as a riding instructor, the two enjoy participating in various equine and rodeo events together, including team roping. They live in Granite Bay, California.